I0620923

The Relic

Also by Jeff Lowe:

The Book of Cain

JEFF LOWE

The Relic

Little White Cain, LLC
Woodland, Alabama

Copyright © 2019 by Jeff Lowe

All rights reserved.

All rights reserved. No part of this publication may be reproduced, distributed, or transmitted in any form or by any means, including photocopying, recording, or other electronic or mechanical methods, without the prior written permission of the publisher, except in the case of brief quotations embodied in critical reviews and certain other noncommercial uses permitted by copyright law. For permission requests, write to the publisher at the address below.

Little White Cabin, LLC
197 County Road 531
Woodland, AL 36280
publisher@littlewhitecabin.com

To James W. Lowe
my father

God bless the Old Man, Master, Mate, and Pilot
Receive him into your safe and eternal harbor
Let him sail his ship and shoot the stars
Let him smell the salt spray and feel the swell again
Let him walk the bridge and the windy wing
Let him feel the pure love of his wife and his family
The respect of his crew, the admiration of his friends
The gratitude of every stranger whose life he uplifted
The last bell has tolled on his earthly watch,
He stood it well and strong
Give him fair winds and following seas
Forever and ever.
Amen.

Chapters

1. Chick's Gift

THE OLD MAN SLUMPED DEEP IN THE ARMCHAIR that sat in the middle of the common room in the Safe Haven homeless shelter. An ancient pea coat, big enough to fit a man twice his size, draped like a tent over the dry twigs of his frame, and an old sea captain's hat covered his bald head with the brim settled on the bridge of his nose. His snores mixed with the sounds coming from two television sets on the wall, one tuned to a news channel, the other to cartoons, and he did not notice the snaggle-toothed woman creep toward him.

She wore layers upon layers of ragged, mismatched clothes that swished and chafed as she moved. Her clodhopper boots had no laces, the tongues flopped out and the soles scraped and clomped, and with every footfall the wooden floor squeaked, and yet no one turned to look at her, other than a ten-year-old girl who had been watching the cartoons. Nor did the snaggle-toothed woman look at them. Her eyes fixed on the pink envelope lying on the slumbering old man's chest.

Standing over him, she glanced at his face. His eyes twitched under the lids and his lips and Adam's apple jerked as if he was trying to call for help or maybe he was drowning. She thought he could wake up pretty quick from a dream like that, so she pinched the envelope and made for the Christmas tree in the back corner of the room.

In her glee she cackled with laughter and tripped over a chair, and everyone except the old man turned to look at her as she crashed to the floor. The girl started yelling, "Miss Bernice! Miss Bernice! Miss Bernice! Sissy's stealing Chick's gift! Miss Bernice!"

A middle-aged woman in overalls flung the swinging door open and entered the common room from the kitchen. "What's all the racket about?" she said, wiping her hands on a dishtowel. "Why are you yelling, Monica?"

Monica was hopping up and down and pointing at the thief, who was now trying to squeeze behind the Christmas tree in the corner of the room. "Miss Bernice, Sissy's stealing Chick's Christmas present! Go see! Go see!"

The Christmas tree fell over with a shush of plastic needles and the tiny, high-pitched crash of shattering ornaments, leaving Sissy standing there with her hands behind her back crying out, "I ain't stole nothing, you little liar!"

The commotion jerked the old man from his sleep and he lurched out of his chair and stood there with his feet spread and his arms up like a woozy boxer, blinking and wheezing, "What? What's going on?" as he struggled to orient himself in the world beyond his dreams.

Miss Bernice put her fists on her hips and scowled at the thief. "Sissy! Remember what we talked about? You can't stay at Safe Haven if you steal people's things. Now hand it over."

Sissy jerked the envelope from behind her back and clutched it against her shoulder. "No, it's mine!"

"It's not yours, Sissy, it's Chick's," Monica said. "You stole it. I saw you."

"Nuh-uh, I didn't steal it, Chick give it to me. He said I could have it as a Christmas present. Chick and me are lovers like Adam and Eve, like Rodeo and Joliet, like... like Sodom and Gomorrah! We share!"

Miss Bernice turned to the old man. "Chick?"

"You know it's not true, Miss Bernice," Monica said. "Chick can't stand Sissy, can you, Chick?"

The old man shuffled his feet to keep his balance and shook his head as if he had water in his ears. "What the hell is going on?" he muttered.

"All right," Miss Bernice said and stepped toward Sissy. "Hand it over." The woman clutched the envelope tighter by her ear and pushed back against the wall. "Sissy!" Miss Bernice barked. "Do you want to stay here or not? It's cold outside, you know, but I will not hesitate putting you out on the street again."

Sissy pouted, then smiled and with a little hula wave of her hips said, "I'll give it to Chick if Chick comes and gives me a kiss under the mistletoe."

The old man shuddered and made a face like a baby that had just sucked on a lemon.

"Aw, come on, Chick," Sissy said, "You got a long white beard like Santa. I'll bet it tickles when you kiss—hmmmmwaa..." Her lips moved like worms as she beckoned him with kisses.

"I wouldn't kiss you with Stanley's slimy lips," Chick said, frowning.

A man watching the TV with the news program on it twisted around and said, "Hey! To hell with you, you old fascist!" One side of his face drooped and spittle foamed in the turned-down corner of his mouth.

"Don't you call my man names, Stanley... not-so-hot-to-Trotsky, you drooling old communist!" Sissy said. "I wouldn't kiss you either, not with... not with... not with a dead cat's lips, not for a million billion bucks."

Stanley stood and jabbed his finger in the air. "You damn capitalist pigs and your greed! You think about nothing but money! You see that child standing there? No child should be in a place like this! It is a crime for any child to starve or to live on the street! A crime against humanity! Socialism is the only way! Now you morons be quiet. We educated people want to watch the news." Stanley's stroke made it hard for him to say his "s" and "f" sounds without slobbering and gumming up the sounds of his favorite words, and a young man on the other side of the room mocked him with a steady stream of farting and slurping noises. Stanley flipped him the bird as he wiped his mouth with his sleeve, then turned and plopped back into his chair.

"All right, that's enough," Miss Bernice said. She held her hand toward Sissy. "Hand it over or hit the bricks. Now."

Sissy sighed and rolled her eyes, then slapped the envelope into Miss Bernice's hand and slid down the wall to sit on the floor in a limp, sobbing puddle.

Miss Bernice studied the writing on the envelope. "Where did this come from?" she said.

"Santa brought them early this morning when everybody was asleep but me," Monica said. "I was up. He gave them to me to hand out. Everybody got one. I got twenty dollars in mine. Look." She waved the bill in the air. When the others saw that, they rushed to find and tear open their envelopes.

"Monica," Miss Bernice said, "this isn't your handwriting..."

"Oh no, Miss Bernice, it's Santa's. He had already put everybody's name on them. He just gave me the stack and asked me to hand them out."

Miss Bernice rubbed her forehead and sighed. "Look, Monica, this is very nice, but you know you're not supposed to be letting anyone in without my permission. It could be very dangerous, dear."

"Oh, I didn't let him in," Monica said. "He just opened the door and walked right in."

"But... I'm sure I locked that door last night. No one else has a key."

Monica laughed. "Santa doesn't need a key, Miss Bernice, you silly goose!"

"Monica, what did this man look like?"

The girl frowned comically. "Everybody knows what Santa looks like," she said. "He's got a long white beard and white hair, kinda like Chick, but he's really big, and Chick's not. Chick's kinda scrawny. Everybody was asleep but me, I was writing my letter to Santa, so I gave it to him after he gave me the gifts. Wasn't that nice?"

"But... how did he know everybody's name?" Miss Bernice said. "How did he know all these people were here?"

"Gosh, Miss Bernice! You don't know much about Santa Claus!"

The woman studied the envelope in her hands and peered at the old man. "Chick, does anybody know you're here? I mean, anybody who knows you well, from your past, maybe?"

The old man shrugged. "I'm a nobody. A bum. Nobody knows where I am or cares what I do, 'specially one that has money to hand out."

She showed him the front of the envelope. "Is this your full name?"

"I don't have my reading glasses," he said.

"It says Chickamauga Antietam Charles."

The old man stared at her with his mouth open.

"I knew it had to be Chick," Monica said. "There was Chick and there was Charles, and I took the middle stuff out and there it was: Chick Charles. I'm good at being a detective. I put it on his chest when he was sleeping."

"All right," Miss Bernice said. "This isn't the first time an anonymous benefactor has passed out Christmas gifts here. I just wish they'd come to me first. Here, Chick, you may as well get your twenty bucks."

"Sure," he said, "I'll just rip it right open. Better yet I'll chew it open. Lemme just put in my choppers."

"Oh, can I do it for you?" Monica said, and she took the envelope from Miss Bernice and carefully opened it along the seal. "Hey, look. Chick didn't get money. He got this." She held up the colorful strip of paper.

A young man in a white wife-beater undershirt with tattoos on his shoulders and neck, the one who had mocked Stanley, stood up and yelled, "Hey! That ain't fair! How come that old fart gets a lottery ticket, and we just get twenty bucks?"

"What is wrong with you fools!" Stanley shouted. "The lottery is just another scam the capitalist system uses to keep the working man in chains. It's the new religion, an opiate of the masses. You may as well believe in Santa Claus. Fools, I say. That ticket isn't worth the paper it's written on."

"The hell it's not," the young man said. "That's a pick-six. That thing's worth thousands, man, probably five grand! Hey old man, tell you what, I'll buy that ticket from you. Trade you my twenty, straight up. Come on, that's a two-dollar ticket, and you didn't spend a dime on it."

"And what would you do with five thousand dollars, Paulie?" Miss Bernice said to the young man.

"I could do a damn sight better than the methadone I been doing," he said. "It's like Stanley said, man, masses of opiates! Come on, Chick-a-chuck, twenty bucks for your pick-six."

"Don't do it, Chick," Monica said. "Santa gave you that ticket. You'll win. The lottery comes on the cartoon channel, I see it every morning. Look, here it is!"

She pointed to the TV and everyone but Stanley turned to look. "You morons keep your foolishness to yourselves, and be quiet while I watch the news," he said. "We educated people would rather... Oh, and wouldn't you know it! Speaking of opiates of the masses! Look at this so-called documentary on the so-called news station! Fascist Christians on a pilgrimage to a fascist church in Bolonia, which by the way is in fascist Spain, which by the way is still ruled by the ghost of the fascist dictator Franco, and look at them! Just look at them! What is it with Catholics and their relics? Praying to a bunch of bones, for God's sake! Fools! Superstitious fools, just like all of you and your Merry Christmases and your Santa Clauses and your lottery tickets. Look at them, believing that the fossils of some old so-called saint will cure them of their cleft palates and their spina bifida and God-knows-what-else. They should be forming a picket line to drum all these spiritual hucksters out of town, but no, no, no, no, instead they're lining up like Paulie and his friends at the methadone clinic to pray to a box of dust in the... the what?... ah, the Church of the Santo Remero! Hah! What a crock!" He wiped a prodigious amount of drool from his chin.

The old man shuddered and turned to look at the TV that Stanley was watching. "Santo Remero," he whispered.

"The first number's a one!" Monica yelled. "You got that one, Chick!"

The old man stared bug-eyed at the TV screen. The reporter was interviewing the priest and a classy-looking older woman on the steps of the church. They were surrounded by pilgrims. The priest was in his vestments and the woman wore a brilliant royal blue dress. Her hair, auburn with streaks of gray, shone in the sun. The woman had a dignified air, somehow both proud and humble, and when she smiled and spoke in broken English, the old man trembled and whispered, "Maria."

"The second one's a two! The second one's a two!" Monica shouted. "You got the first two, Chick!"

The documentary cut to a clip of a doctor treating patients—poor people in shacks and hovels, some in streets and alleys and vacant lots. The doctor's name appeared on the bottom of the screen: Doctor Jack Smith Montoya. The camera returned to the woman, Maria, who smiled and said, "The people call him Doctor Jack. My son." The old man's knees began to buckle.

"Oh wow, Chick, you got the third number!" Monica squealed. It's a two! It's a two! Look, one-two-two!"

On the TV, Maria and the priest led the reporter into the church, down the aisle, and into the sacristy near the back. In that small room there was a table and on the table was a box. Music could be heard. The camera panned to where a young man was standing, playing a

guitar. Maria said the young man's name was Emilio
Santiago.

The old man sucked in a wheezing breath and pointed
to the screen. "That's... That's my... That's my..." He
shook his head and blinked when he realized the young
man was playing a Spanish-flavored version of the old
Gene Autry tune "Here Comes Santa Claus."

"It's a five! It's a five! Everybody, it's a five! Chick,
that's four in a row! Only two left!" Monica was
bouncing up and down on her toes.

"Old man!" Paulie barked. "Twenty five bucks for
your ticket! I got twenty here and I'll owe you five, swear
to God, I'll pay up tomorrow! Come on, dude, it ain't
gonna hit the last two, it never does, ain't that right,
Stanley? Huh? This is just something to keep the
working man down, right, Stanley? Come on, old man...
OK, thirty! Stanley, tell him! He ain't gonna win!"

But even Stanley the socialist had risen from his chair
and was intently watching the lottery on the cartoon
channel.

The old man stepped toward the TV with the
documentary and paid no attention to the lottery. The
priest said, "The sacrifice of El Santo Remero was
responsible for both the amazing surgical prowess of the
good Doctor Jack and the miraculous healings
experienced by these pilgrims upon contact with the
holy relics. It is the true meaning of the laying on of
hands." As the priest reached for the latch on the box,
the old man's forearms began to twitch with painful
spasms.

"Oh my God, oh my God, oh my God it's a six!" Monica shrieked. "Chick! Chick, you got five in a row! There's only one left! Here it comes! Hush, everybody!"

The young guitarist strummed chords in a dramatic crescendo as the priest lifted the lid of the box and the camera zoomed and focused on the relics inside. The old man's jaw dropped and a wheezy, gurgly groan escaped from somewhere deep in his chest as he raised his arm and staggered backward into Miss Bernice.

"Zero! Aaaahhh! One-two-two-five-six-zero, Chick, you won!" Monica and the others in the little crowd whooped and clapped, except for Paulie, who was glaring at the old man and shaking his head, and Stanley, who was trying to explain to everyone how it was all a scam and how Chick ought to distribute his unearned income equally among the oppressed masses of the Safe Haven homeless shelter.

Miss Bernice had lowered the old man onto the floor as gently as she could and fanned his face. "My gosh," she said. "He's fainted. Who would've thought that crusty old sailor would ever get that excited about winning a little money."

"It's not just a little money," Monica said, pointing to the TV. "Look."

"Well, I'll be," Miss Bernice said. "That's a lot of money. Wonder what he'll do with it." She extended her hand toward the girl. "Monica, honey, we need to put that in a safe place, hand it to me and..."

With an angry growl, Paulie rushed by and snatched the lottery ticket from Monica's hand, jumped over the slumped body of the old man, raced for the front door, threw it open and was gone.

Sissy let out a wail and clomped after him as fast as her floppy boots and mounds of clothes would let her go. To everyone's surprise she came shuffling back less than a minute later. She stood there, eyes wide and mouth agape as if she had seen a ghost. Then she raised her hand and looked at the lottery ticket she was holding.

"You got it back!" Monica shouted. "Yay!" She ran up and hugged the woman.

"Oh, thank God," Miss Bernice said. "Sissy, how'd you do it? What happened?"

Sissy worked her jaws until words came out. "Paulie ran into Santa," she said.

"What?" Miss Bernice jogged to the door and looked out. "I don't see him."

"Santa... told him not to steal Chick's stuff. I think maybe somebody should take Paulie to the 'mergency room. He don't look so good." Sissy shook her head. "He used to have such a nice smile, did Paulie. He just a old snagglepuss like me now."

The old man started thrashing about and the others helped him to his feet and clapped him on the back. "Hey Chick, man, you won the lottery!... Whatcha gonna do with all that cash, dude?... You ain't gonna forget your friends at the Safe Haven, are you?... How 'bout spreading the wealth a little, like, you know, it's Christmas, right?... It's the season for charity... Hey, remember when I let you have the rest of my soup?... Equal distribution among the people, comrade!... Chick, man, you should be happy! You look like you seen the devil, you OK, man?... Chick, what's wrong?"

The old man stood there with his feet spread and his knees bent as if straining to keep his balance on the deck of a ship tossed by heavy seas. He pointed at the TV. He shook. He wheezed and he grunted and finally the words came tumbling out: "I... I... I got to go... I got to go NOW!"

"What're you talking about, Chick? Where you got to go, man?"

He glared at Miss Bernice in a strange panic, his face twisting and twitching as if the tectonic plates of his soul were grinding out of their long-settled position. He hissed out a slobbery "S" sound before emitting a long groan of "pain."

2. Church of El Santo Remero

THE OLD MAN STEPPED OUT OF HIS HIRED CAR into a throng of pilgrims crowding the street in front of the church in Bolonia. He knew that the driver, who spoke perfectly good tourist-trap English, had pinched more than the offered tip when he asked him to reach into his pea coat pocket for the fare, but the old man didn't care. He had learned long ago to take a hands-off attitude toward the liberties people took with his condition. Besides, it was Christmas.

Despite his name, Chickamauga Antietam Charles was not a combative person by nature. But looking up those stone steps toward the church, knowing what lay within, he felt a grim determination mixed with a mysterious awe, and so he took a step, and then another. To screw up his courage he resolved not to pussyfoot, but gave each step a little stomp as he ascended. He imagined himself a prizefighter walking up the aisle through a jeering crowd and into the boxing ring.

But he had not gotten even halfway up when one of the pilgrims grabbed his sleeve and jerked him around. They were jabbering in Spanish, shoving him, waving their hands and pointing to the end of the line, far down the street.

"Leave me be," he said. "I ain't no damn pilgrim. What they've got is mine, and I've come to claim it. Now make way." With that, he took another step, and the pilgrim who had grabbed his coat now shoved him hard enough to knock him down, then stood back and raised his fists, boxer-style, bobbing and weaving and taunting the old man. Others in the crowd raised a ruckus, egging him on.

The old man struggled to a standing position, and assumed his own boxing stance. His huge pea coat flapped about his wiry frame and as he pushed his sea captain's hat back on his head and held his arms in a fighting position, his sleeves drooped down and the audience gasped and backed away. His antagonist dropped his guard and stared at the old man as if concussed. "El Santo Remero," he whispered.

The name journeyed from one pilgrim to the next in whispers and shouts until the line melted away and the crowd flowed like lava around the old man with a sound that grew from murmur to raucous din. Soon the priest in his vestments pushed down through the crowd from the top of the stairs, yelling at people and jabbing with his shepherd's crook to open a path.

When he got there the priest urged the crowd to back away and he gave the old man a look of stern authority and said something in Spanish.

The old man was wheezing, fearful of the crowd but more resolved than ever to do what he came to do, and he said, "I seen you on the TV, preacher. You got something that's mine, and I want it back."

The priest furrowed his brow and studied the old man. "You are American?" he said.

"Damn right, and don't you forget it."

"I am Father Carlos. What is your name?"

"I'm Jack Smith," he said, pronouncing each syllable with a defiant clarity. The old man was secretly relieved that the priest spoke such good English, and even more relieved that he had not come to blows with the rash young pilgrim.

"Well then... welcome to Bolonia." The priest hesitated before speaking again. "You will forgive my skepticism, Mr. Smith, but we have in the past had problems with people pretending to be... well, Jack Smith. You see, the world is full of imposters and... how do you say in America, 'con men' who scheme to profit from the suffering of others." He swept his arm to show he was referring to the pilgrims.

"That's your problem, not mine," the old man said.

The priest frowned. "Well, sir, let me inform you how we have dealt with this problem. We have passed laws here. Laws that punish con men and imposters who would prey on these poor pilgrims. And you, sir, do not seem to have the—how shall I say?—the servant's heart or the humble manner of El Santo Remero." He said something in Spanish and two men among the pilgrims grabbed the old man by the arms while a third dug into the pockets of his pea coat. He pulled out a passport and handed it to the priest.

Father Carlos opened it, then glanced at the old man. "This says your name is Cheeka-ma-ooga Antee-et-am Charles. Not Jack Smith. I am calling the police."

As the priest dug into his own pocket for his cell phone a woman shouted from the top of the stairs, and everyone turned to look at her. The crowd parted like the Red Sea for Moses as she descended. With her bright yellow dress and shimmering, gray-streaked auburn hair, she looked to the old man like a beautiful flower in a field of drab weeds. As she neared him, she stopped and studied him from several steps above. Then she smiled, skipped down the remaining steps and threw her arms around his neck.

"Mi Santo Remero," she cried, and a joyous shout went up from the crowd, while many of the pilgrims dropped to their knees and crossed themselves.

She let go of his neck and looked deep into his eyes. "I search for you many years," she said. "I never can find you. I have friends, young people, look for you on, how you say, Internet, and no. Nothing. There must be a million of Jack Smith in America. So finally, my son, he is doctor, he say old people like us watch television, and so, we put on television, and... here you are!"

"You speak... English?" the old man said.

She laughed. "Now, yes, a little. Not... how you say? Not in past. I learn for you. For you, Jack Smith, my hero, my Santo Remero." She turned and held his arm above the elbow. "Come," she said, "we go into church." As they ascended, woman on one arm, priest on the other, Maria said, "You must meet my son. I name him for you. He is doctor. He has hands to save people. Like you, my Santo Remero, like you. He is out helping young woman with difficult birth now. You see him after."

As they ascended the steps, many of the pilgrims reached out to touch the old man's pea coat, then crossed themselves. This bothered him, not just because religious "mumbo-jumbo," as he called it, always seemed foreign and weird to him, but he knew from experience that beggars and pickpockets go together like stray cats and fleas, and these pilgrims had a beggarly look about them. It was bad enough they had things in the church that belonged to him. There were things in his pockets—and not just the lottery cash—that he needed and he didn't want to part with. He began to worry that, not only would he fail to reclaim his things, they'd seize what he had left and use them for relics, too.

Maria's touch and voice were making him giddy, though, and the chip on his shoulder seemed to shrink with each step, from a brick to a pack of smokes, a single cigarette, a butt, an ash, a wisp of memory. After six steps he felt light, as if Maria and Father Carlos were carrying him up the stairs, and if they let go, he'd float up into the blue Andalusian sky like a balloon.

With a worshipful bow, two pilgrims swung open the tall oaken doors and the three entered the church. Maria and the priest knelt and crossed themselves while the old man stood and blinked to adjust his eyes to the dim light. As they walked together slowly down the aisle between the pews, Maria hugged the old man's arm and spoke in a stage whisper—so close to his ear he could feel her warm breath—telling him story after story of surgical and miraculous healings that never would have happened without him, her Santo Remero.

He recognized the door to the sacristy from having seen it on the documentary and suddenly he felt heavier. His shoes began to scrape on the floor and he found himself being pulled along, more like a reluctant donkey than a balloon. The sacristy door was open. He stopped at the threshold and hesitated as if at a cattle guard.

Suddenly his heart started to pound and he found it hard to breathe. "Maybe I shouldn't have come," he said, choking, and he turned away from the door.

Then he heard the guitar play. The notes were pure, the sound sublime. He stopped and listened. He started to cry. Gently, Maria placed her hand on his cheek and pressed his other cheek to hers. Their tears mingled. He turned and she guided him slowly into the sacristy.

The young man with the guitar bowed his head toward the old man as he played. Maria said, "This is Emilio. He is Santiago's grandson. You remember Santiago, yes?"

The old man nodded.

"Santiago came to me in a dream," she said. "He said, Maria, the cabin boy wanders the earth in sorrow and loneliness. You must find him. Tell him of our love for him. Tell him of our..." she looked at the priest.

"Gratitude," the priest said.

"Tell him of our gratitude," Maria said. "Bring him home to Bolonia, Maria. He is a saint. He is our saint. Heal his sorrow. Show him, Maria. Show him the

holiness of his sacrifice. Show him the truth." She slid
her hand down his arm to his wrist and gently squeezed.
"I look for you many, many years. I pray for this
moment."

She took her hand from his arm and grasped the
corner of the box lid. The priest put his hand on the
other corner. The old man wanted to say "wait," he
wasn't ready, he wanted to retrieve the little bottle from
a secret pocket in his pea coat, the little bottle with the
faded handwritten label. It had stayed there, hidden for
decades, through feast and famine, sobriety and
drunkenness and delirium tremens, and now he needed
it, now was the time for it, but his palpitating heart was
lodged in his throat and he couldn't say a word.

3. A Christmas Wish

"OH, YOU WANT TO KNOW MY WISH, HUH?"
The kid's growl rolled out too quiet for the other riders on the bus to hear. They were all bundled up against the bitter cold and sleet, yet he was without coat or hat. The ice that had pelted him in the slicing wind outside had melted in the relative warmth of the bus. Even so, he was cold and damp and beginning to shiver, though he didn't yet realize it. Humiliation burns hot and long when you're sixteen.

He was sitting on a bench leaning forward with his elbows on his knees and his hands out in front of him, palms up, fingers slightly curled and trembling. He had been glaring at them like a judge condemning traitors to execution until he got so disgusted he looked up and saw the poster. It was an advertisement for Puller's department store showing a jolly Santa who asked, "What's your Christmas wish?"

The second time, it was in the bark of an angry dog. "So you really want to know what I wish, you old bastard?" Some of the other riders looked at him.

He had been playing the scene over and over again in his mind. At the party, that beautiful girl, the one he had a crush on, the one with the chestnut hair pulled back in a pony tail, the one with the pretty blue eyes and the dazzling smile: Celeste, the one he had always liked but they had only been friends—the "You Don't Know Me" kind of friends—but not anymore. No, at this Christmas party he was going to bust out of his shell, and he had practiced, night and day for weeks he had practiced, and at home he was great, he was smooth, he was oh-so-virtuoso—the way his fingers danced on the strings, the way his voice rolled through the lyrics—and this night he would take that risk, he would throw caution to the wind and show her who he really was. And he was going to play "You Don't Know Me," not like Eddy Arnold, not like Jerry Vale, but like and as himself, and his version would be hers because it would open her eyes and her heart to the real Chick Charles.

But there at the party in front of Celeste and everyone else watching him—and worse yet, listening to him—it felt as if his hands had turned to hooves and he couldn't make a single good note or chord on that damned guitar, and his heart pounded and his throat choked up and on top of it all he forgot the lyrics. Everything fell apart, everything! And as he slunk off to the wall amid the polite, pitiful clapping, he heard an old woman say, "Aw, bless his heart!" and the words stung like a hornet. He turned once to look back and there was Celeste in the center of the room but she wasn't looking back at him with any pity or compassion or anything else because Gerard, her real-life boyfriend, tall, handsome Gerard had her in his arms and kissed her on the lips under the mistletoe and everybody cheered and she said, "Well, Merry Christmas to me!" and she was beaming. Absolutely beaming. And so Chick Charles walked out the door without his hat or coat or even his guitar, and he started to run through the bitter, icy night, and he didn't stop until he hopped on that city bus.

He didn't even know where it was going. And he didn't watch where it went, either. He just sat there as the bus wheezed and rumbled along, glaring at his hands with the kind of burning hatred only a humiliated teenager can feel. And the third time he yelled it in a maniac rage, "You want to know what I wish, old man? Huh? I wish you would just take these god-damned hands! Just take them away, they're no use to me! God damn you all to hell!"

Puller's Santa didn't look at him any different, but the few other riders left on the bus did, and the driver yelled back, "Hey! Watch your mouth, kid, or you can just get off this bus, got it?"

The kid heard him but paid him no mind. He was imagining being back at the party and somehow chopping both his hands off with an axe and spraying the entire crowd with his hot, spurting blood, and he could just see Celeste there, Celeste with the movie star dreams, drenched in his blood, and Gerard too, and he had the weird thought that someday somebody should make a movie about the king and queen of the high school prom getting drenched in blood and he cackled like a hyena at the stupidity of it all.

The bus squealed to a stop and the driver called out, "End of the line. Everybody off the bus." Chick woke from his fantasy and looked around. He was the only rider left. The door swung open. The cold wind blew in. He could hear the ice pellets tinking on the side of the bus and the sidewalk. He hesitated.

"End of the line," the driver said again. "Get off the bus."

"Uhh... Where are we?" the kid said.

"First Avenue and Dockside," the driver said. "End of the line."

"Well, how do I get back?"

"Next bus is 6 a.m. You can either wait for it or call yourself a cab."

It was well below freezing. The wind and sleet were getting worse. There was no way he could stand out in the street all night without so much as a coat or hat. "Can't I just wait on the bus?" he said.

"No. You gotta get off. That's the rules. Look, there's a pay phone about a block down the street. Go call yourself a ride."

He glanced at the Santa poster. "To hell with you," he said, and stepped off the bus.

The driver called out, "Oh, and Merry Christmas to you too, ya little jerk." The doors swished shut and the bus lurched away with a wheezy rumble, its tires crunching on the pellets of ice that were starting to coat the street.

The kid hugged himself, canted his head against the piercing ice needles and began jogging down the street.

At the end of the first block he slipped on ice and fell, scraping one knee and the palms of his hands. He limped onward. Near the end of the second block he saw the phone booth in the distance, and he picked up his pace again. He was desperate to get inside, to close the door behind him and find some sanctuary from the brutal chill. He stuck his hands in his pockets to try to feel for some coins, but his fingers were already starting to go numb. He was afraid he wouldn't be able to count the coins or put them in the phone.

It didn't matter anyway. The phone booth had no door, nor any walls. The glass sides were shattered and lying on the sidewalk and in the gutter. He couldn't tell the difference between the glass shards and the ice. And the phone's handset wasn't even there. Just wires hanging out with loose ends, swaying in the wind.

He hurried down the street, along a row of ancient brick buildings of the kind you find near the docks, pushing on every door he came to, but they were all locked and dark. There was no traffic in the street—no buses, no cabs, no cars or trucks. He turned back toward where the bus let him off, but that was into the wind, so he turned around again to keep the wind to his back. He wandered, increasingly desperate and afraid, into side streets and alleys, but he found no protection from the cold. His gait became stiff and clumsy as he lost feeling in his feet, and when he could not feel his ears or his cheeks, he began to fret that he was actually going to die out there.

He tried to yell for help, but his upper body had become wracked with spasms as the heat drained from his core, and his voice tumbled out weak and unheard. He slipped on ice and fell again. He tried to rise, once, twice, and then just lay there in disbelief that he was actually going to freeze to death. And then he heard someone yell. A man's voice. Not yelling, really, but singing, loud and boisterous. He pushed up onto his hands and knees and looked down the street.

He saw a man in the yellow gloom of a streetlamp at the end of the next block. The kid locked his eyes on him. He staggered to his feet and stumbled toward the light, trying to yell as he went. When he got there, he saw it was an old man with a white beard. His oversized pea coat was unbuttoned and flapping in the wind as he spun around in his happy dance. His sea captain's hat, also too large for him, flopped on his head.

He laughed gaily as he sang, and didn't appear in the least cold. As the kid stumbled to him, the old man spread his arms, smiled and grasped him in a bear hug. "Why, my boy, you're shaking like a leaf," he said, and he stepped back and shook off his coat. Then he draped it around the kid's shoulders, placed the sea captain's hat on his head and stood back with his fists on his hips, considering him.

"There," the old man said. "Shipshape." His wispy hair and beard flapped with the wind. Tiny icicles gathered in his whiskers. He inhaled deeply through his nostrils and, looking about with a grin, said, "Ain't it grand, boy?" He danced some more steps and then stopped, facing the dock across the street.

"Christmas in Tahiti! The warm sands! The clear waters! The pretty girls!" He sniffed the air. "Aahhh, can you smell it, boy? Yaaah, that pig's been roasting there under the sand for a day and a night, tender and juicy, wrapped in banana leaves. Are you hungry, boy?" And with that, the old man danced into the street, skating here and there on the ice, and then he was on the other side, on the dock.

The kid could hardly see him now through the sleet and tears in his eyes. The old man yelled something that got whisked away in the wind, and then he was gone. There was a splash, and then nothing but the wind and the tinking of the sleet. The kid stood there for a few seconds, then stumbled across the street and dropped to his knees at the edge of the dock.

"Old man!" he yelled, his voice shaking with the tremors in his chest. He blinked and rubbed his eyes but the lamplight was dim here and he could see nothing in the water below. He could hear the sound of wind-whipped waves and the crackle of foam and the crunch of ice that had begun to form around the pier, but no splashing of a man trying to swim, and no call for help.

"Old man!" he cried out again. "Oh my God," he whispered. He stood and staggered back across the dock and the street, clutching the coat around himself, as his fingers were numb and he couldn't button it. He tried to call for help but his voice died in his convulsing chest.

As he turned a corner onto a side street, he briefly heard voices, and a door slam. He saw lights in a window and a small neon sign flickered once and went dark again. The kid shuffled and slid toward it. As he reached the place, the neon sign crackled and buzzed and flickered again. It said "Seamen's Club."

He tried to turn the doorknob but he couldn't get a grip with his numb hands. He hammered the door weakly with his fists and kicked it with his shoes, but he couldn't seem to make a good knock. He slipped on the ice and fell to his knees on the stoop and his face smacked against the door.

When it opened he flopped face down on the floor. "It's the Old Man," someone said, and pulled him fully into the room and slammed shut the door. When he turned the kid over, he said, "What the... Hey Chief, it ain't the Old Man... it's some kid. He's wearing the Old Man's coat and hat."

"Bring him here, Mr. Sanderson," the Chief said.

The man dragged the kid by the shoulders of his pea coat across the room to a table, then lifted him like a sack of wheat and plopped him on a chair. Across the table the Chief sat with his arms folded over his chest, leaning back in his chair. His khakis were clean but not starched, and his thin, oily hair was combed over a bald spot. His shaven face had the pallor of someone who had spent most of his life in a cave. He studied the kid through black-rimmed glasses.

"Where's the Old Man?" he said.

The kid tried to speak, but his chest was still shaking from the cold and he sounded like a little motor that was coughing and unable to start.

The Chief leaned forward and laid his elbows on the table, his fingers intertwined, and studied his subject. Then he turned his head and said, "Bartender, bring the boy a cup of your chicken soup. Warm, not hot. He seems to be suffering a touch of hypothermia."

As the bartender prepared the soup, the kid glanced around the room. The light was dim but it seemed to him there were about six other people there: the man who met him at the door, the Chief, the bartender, two other men—one sitting at the table and one standing— and a figure slumped in the shadows in the back of the room, who seemed to be covered with a blanket or shawl.

The bartender brought the cup of soup and set it in front of the kid. It looked and smelled to him like life itself. He placed his shaking hands on either side of the cup and made to lift it, but the Chief set his hand over the top and pressed down. Then he dragged the cup to the middle of the table, away from the kid. The Chief then pulled a small vial from his shirt pocket. The cap was an eyedropper. He unscrewed it and held the eyedropper over the cup, then squeezed drops of a clear liquid into the soup. "A little elixir to warm the core and loosen the tongue," he said, and pushed the cup of soup back to the kid. "There. Drink up."

The kid looked at the cup suspiciously, then at the others in the room. They looked back at him with mute, expectant expressions. Then the man who dragged him from the front door, Sanderson, bent over and said in his ear, "We're seamen, young fella. We make our living out on ships, where there ain't no doctors or nothing. We gotta take care of ourselves when we get, you know..." he looked at the Chief, who said "hypothermia."

"Yeah, that," Sanderson said. "So we're used to doctoring ourselves. What the Chief give you, that's just medicine. We've all took it time and again when we've needed it. It works, guaranteed. Warm you right up. And the Chief there, he's a engineer, so he knows what it's all about scientifically, you know. He's real smart— knows a lot about a lot. You can trust him to doctor you up good."

"Go on, drink it," the Chief said. "You'll feel better."

So the kid drank the soup, and though he could not taste the elixir, his shaking began to subside and a bit of warmth seeped back into his chest.

"Now," the Chief said, "let's try this again. That coat and hat don't belong to you. So tell me: how did you come about them?"

"I was lost... and... and cold... and... and I... I saw him..."

"What did he look like?"

"Umm... He... he had... a white... a white beard, and..."

"What was he doing when you saw him?"

"He... he was... umm... singing and... I don't know... dancing, I... I guess, and... he... he saw I was... I was cold, and... he gave me his coat... and... and his hat..."

"And where was this?"

The kid pointed back toward the front door. His arm was shaking. "Down that way... a couple of... blocks, I guess... by the waterfront."

"What happened then? Is he still there, or did he go somewhere?"

"He... he..." the kid broke down in sobs. "I... I tried to..."

"Relax, boy, just tell me what you saw. Where did he go?"

"He... he... he danced... across the street and... and he... he fell."

"Fell. What do you mean, fell?"

"He fell off the dock... into the water... I tried... I tried to see... I couldn't reach..."

The Chief leaned forward. "What the hell are you talking about, boy? Did you say he fell into the water?"

"I didn't see him... I didn't see him come back up," the kid blubbered. "I think he... I think he drowned. I came... to look... for help."

The men looked at each other. "Sanderson, Randolph," the Chief barked. "Run out there to the dock, see what you can see. Hurry!" The two men ran out of the room.

When the door slammed, the figure in the back, which until then seemed to have been sleeping head-down on a table in the shadows, suddenly stood and approached them. The voice coming from within the hood was female, and chattering in a foreign language. She sounded worried, angry, insistent. Then she threw off her scarf and grabbed the kid by his coat lapels as if demanding to know the same thing the Chief Engineer wanted to know: what happened to the Old Man.

The kid judged her to be about his own age, and as stunning as a bird of prey, with flowing auburn hair and dark eyes burning with a passion that both intimidated and enchanted him. Despite her youth, he sensed there was something terribly mature or experienced about her, and then he realized what it was. As one of the men pulled her away from the kid, she slapped at him and then placed her hands on her belly, pregnant and far along with child.

As the man nudged her farther from the table she turned and kicked him in the shin, then slapped his cheek. The man raised his hand as if to strike her, but the Chief barked, "Benson! You will do no such thing. She must not be harmed." He turned toward the bar. "Bartender, tell Maria everything is all right. Tell her the Old Man just lent his coat to a lost boy. He'll be around by and by."

"Chief, my Spanish ain't too good, you know."

"It's a simple message. Use simple words. Everything is all right. The Old Man will be back soon. He will take her to the sanctuary, as promised. But first he wants us to meet him back on the ship."

"He does?" Benson said.

"As far as she is concerned, Mr. Benson, yes, he does. Tell her, Bartender." Just then the two other men returned from their foray into the storm. The Chief motioned them to his table and gestured for them to speak quietly so that Maria could not hear. "Well, gentlemen, what did you find?"

"Looks like the kid's telling the truth," Sanderson said. "We found his footprints in the sleet, the way it built up on the ground, you know? Looks like he danced across the street, like the kid says, and the prints go to the edge of the dock and then they don't go nowheres else. It's scraped there like he lost his footing."

"I shined my flashlight down in the water, Chief," Randolph said. "The ice has done started to build around the piers already." He glanced at Maria and lowered his voice. "Looks to me like he fell through, and didn't come back up. You know that Christmas card in the pink envelope he likes to give out to hobos and waitresses and whatnot? It was down there, on the ice. I seen it. Like he dropped it when he fell. He's done for, Chief, I'm sure of it. Ain't no other explanation."

The Chief Engineer pressed his fingertips together against his lips and nodded. He looked at the kid. "Would you say, boy, that the Old Man looked drunk, or sober, when you saw him?"

"I don't know, drunk, I guess," he said. "He was talking like... like he was in Tahiti, I think he said. It was like... he wasn't cold at all."

The Chief nodded again. "I see." He shook his head and a smile crept onto his face. "It is a sad tale indeed," he said, "when a man accustomed to peppermint schnapps instead imbibes something a bit more... oh, how shall I say? Profound." He snapped his fingers.

"Bartender, whiskey for my crew and a ginger ale for me."

As the bartender went about his order, the kid said, "But... aren't you going to call the police, or... an ambulance, or something?" The Chief Engineer and the others laughed and didn't answer him. They snickered and elbowed each other like they had just won a secret game. The kid looked desperately from one to the other, confused by their strange response to the drowning of their shipmate.

The bartender set out the drinks, and the Chief lifted his glass. "Gentlemen! A toast. To the gratitude a certain someone will show us upon the return of his..." he made a subtle glance in the direction of the pregnant woman, "very valuable property." The others drained their glasses and resumed their secretive celebration.

The kid said, "Thanks for your help, but I need to go home now. Can I use a phone to call a cab... or something? Excuse me, but can I use a phone?"

He looked at the young woman. She was sitting at the table in the back again, in the shadows with her head covered. The bartender was leaning over her, speaking softly, patting her on the shoulder, and nodding his head, as if persuading her that everything would be all right, and not to make a fuss.

The kid stood to try to get the men's attention, but his legs felt rubbery and he had to sit down again. He was no longer cold. In fact, he was beginning to sweat. The sounds and lights in the room got loud and colorful and danced like spirits. He felt as if he was about to float out of his seat. He moved, or the room moved, he couldn't tell which, and he was swept out into the night. He found himself back on the bus. The Puller's department store Santa was driving the bus, and the smoke from his pipe wafted back to where he was sitting, and it smelled of peppermint and spruce and Yule logs and tobacco. The bus swayed and rumbled on the rough streets.

He sensed someone sitting close by his side. He turned to look. It was Celeste. He shivered with a warm thrill as she gently caressed his cheek with her fingertips. "Oh, Chick," she breathed into his ear. "My old man." Then she kissed him on the lips and the jostling motion became a smooth, slow swaying as Santa laughed and drove the bus up into the shimmering waves of the northern lights.

4. Jack Smith, Cabin Boy

WHEN HE WOKE UP THE NEXT MORNING he was lying on his back, still wearing the pea coat. He blinked, he wiggled his fingers and toes, and everything felt normal, save for the swaying. It felt strange, as if the ground under him was rocking slowly to and fro. He soon realized he was in a room and he could hear voices. He turned his head toward them, then lay still and listened.

It was the Chief Engineer and the other men he had seen in the seamen's club. But that's not where they were now. It looked to be an office of some kind. There were overhead lights on, but also daylight coming through a window somewhere. He could not follow the conversation the men were having in any detail, but he heard them mention "the kid" once or twice, and "Santiago," and he heard the Chief say, "keep your tongue in your head and your gun under your coat," and then, "when we get to Tangier."

It was that last phrase that made the kid sit bolt upright. He said, "Wait... What?"

The men looked at him. "Go on to your stations," the Chief told the others. "I'll handle this." As the men left he slid a chair to the side of his desk and said, "Get up, boy. Come over here. Sit down... Now." Then he sat down behind the desk and leaned back.

The kid did as he was told. "I... Where are we? I need to go home."

The Chief opened a desk drawer and drew out a sheaf of paper. He held it toward the kid. "This your signature?" he said.

The kid looked at it and said, "Yeah, but I don't..."

The Chief slammed his hand on the desk. "I am the master of this vessel, boy. You will address me as 'Sir' and you will make your responses clear and concise. No 'yeah,' no 'uh-huh.' Now, let's try this again. Is this your signature on this document?"

"Yes, sir. But I..."

"That was a 'yes' or 'no' question, boy. Don't offer more than you're asked. Now I will explain something to you. This document is an employment contract, signed freely by you to serve as cabin boy on this ship. As such your duties will be to do anything I tell you to do. Primarily you will perform duties normally performed by the BR—that is, bedroom steward. You will clean my room and office and you will take care of our passenger, a young woman you may or may not remember from last night. That means you will bring her meals from the galley and you will launder her garments and bedsheets, and bring her any kind of toiletries or other items she may require. And here's what you will not do. You will not tell anyone she is here. You will not mention her name or her presence or give any hint whatsoever to anyone that you are working for anyone but me. Is that clear?"

The kid stared at him with his mouth open.

The Chief opened his desk drawer, pulled out a revolver, calmly raised it at arm's length and gently touched the kid's forehead with the barrel. Then he pulled back the hammer until it clicked. "I said, is that clear?"

"Yes, sir." His cheeks felt hot. His heart was pounding.

The Chief then lowered the hammer and laid the gun on the desk. He adjusted his glasses and held the document at arm's length. "Chickamauga Antietam Charles," he read, then peered at the kid. "A loss and a win for either side. What's its provenance?"

"Sir?"

"Where does it come from? Where'd you get the name?"

"I had relatives... great-great grandfathers, or something, die in those battles. Sir."

"Yankee or Confederate?"

"One of each... sir."

"One of each. A house divided, and all that. Tragic. Well, boy, I will tell you this much. We are going to Tangier, Morocco, and then we will return to the States. If you do exactly as I say, then you will be home in two weeks. Three at the most. If, on the other hand, you screw things up for me, well... Tangier is an old place with old customs. It is a place where they cut the hands off thieves. It is actually quite common to see these

amputees there. I have seen them myself. And if you—
a pale, soft boy unused to the rigors of the Moroccan
street—were to find yourself abandoned in those
quarters, why, I would not be surprised if you soon
found yourself stealing a loaf of bread to satisfy your
hunger, and then, whack! People would be calling you
Stumpy instead of Chickamauga. But then, who knows,
you might be spared the sword. You see, there are still
slave markets in Tangier, where you would likely catch
the eye of a buyer who likes pale soft boys—especially an
American boy, such a prize! And, well... trust me: if you
were to wind up with such a master, you would prefer to
be called Stumpy. Do I make myself clear?"

"Yes, sir."

"Good. Now then. If anyone asks you your name, you
will say it's Jack. Do you understand?"

"Yes, sir."

"What's your name?"

"Jack, sir."

"Jack what?"

"Uhhhh..."

The Chief laughed. "Smith. Let's just say it's Jack
Smith, the cabin boy. But keep it simple. Don't get into
conversations with anyone. Do your job and otherwise
keep to yourself. Now. In a few minutes we will have a
lifeboat drill. It's a regular drill required by the
government for all ships at sea, and all hands must
attend, including you. I want you to be there so the crew
can get used to your presence, and why you're here.

Otherwise keep your mouth shut unless I tell you to open it, do you understand?"

"Yes, sir."

"And remember. The girl does not exist. Understand?"

"What girl, sir?"

"Very good. Smart boy. Intelligent boy. Perhaps you could be an engineer one day." He stood and tucked the revolver under his belt, then put his coat on over it. As they left the captain's office, a crewman opened the door for them and the Chief said, "Are you ready, Benson?" The man pulled back his jacket to show a pistol tucked into his belt, then pulled a blackjack and handcuffs from his back pants pockets. "Good," the Chief said. "Just keep the door closed unless you hear the knock, and do not let her out, do you understand? If you have to restrain her, do so without violence. The sultan will not accept marred merchandise."

5. Lifeboat Drill

"HEY, CHIEF, WHERE IS THE OLD MAN?" Santiago called out. The day engineer was standing in the lifeboat, which was in its gravity davit, while the rest of the crew assigned to it huddled on the deck nearby, hunched in their coats against the brisk wind and sea spray.

"He won't be making this trip," the Chief said.

"Ah, yes," Santiago said with a knowing grin. "I understand. The Old Man, he stay ashore, help Maria. He is good, good Old Man. Santo Viejo! Ole! But Chief, who is captain now?" Santiago spoke with a strong Spanish accent and seemed to the kid to be almost comically cheerful. While the others hunched and grumbled against the cold, their hands stuffed into their coat pockets and their heads squeezed down into their collars, Santiago wore overalls with a sweatshirt underneath and the outer sleeves rolled up, and seemed thoroughly unperturbed by the foul weather.

"I am the acting captain of this vessel, Mr. Santiago."

"You, Chief?" Santiago yelled with a grin. "But you are engineer! Like me! You have license for captain?"

"I am a master mariner, Mr. Santiago. Licensed as master, chief engineer, and radio officer. I could sail this damned ship by myself if I were so inclined. Now get on with it."

Santiago hopped about checking the davits, the cables and fittings, the oars, the lifejackets, the engine, and all with the energy and gracefulness of an acrobat. At some point he noticed the kid. "Hey, boy!" he called. "Who are you? You are new in crew, yes?"

The kid glanced at the Chief. "Jack Smith," he said.

Santiago made a comically exaggerated gesture of cupping his hand to his ear and pressing his finger to his lips and said, "Shhh! Be quiet, wind! Be quiet, waves, I no can hear boy! He has very, very soft voice, like girl."

So the kid yelled out, "Jack Smith, cabin boy."

"Cabin boy?" Santiago said. "Is union position, Chief?"

"No, Mr. Santiago, it's not a union position. Let's just say... Jack is one of the Old Man's charity projects."

Santiago grinned and then pointed at the kid. "Hey! Jack Smith! You have Old Man's coat! And hat! He give to you? You lucky boy! Lucky boy!" After he tested the lifeboat engine, Santiago picked up two long oars and dropped them into their oarlocks. Then he yelled, "I race ship! Ready, set, go!" and gave a dramatic grimace as he vigorously pulled on the oars.

"Come on, Santiago," one of the other crew members yelled, "stop playing around, it's cold out here!"

Santiago laughed and dropped the oars back in their storage racks. "Hey, Chief," he called, "We go to Tangier and no cargo. We go rescue more women, like Maria, hah? Freedom for Christmas, hah?"

Just then a voice cried out that slapped the grin off Santiago's face. It was Maria, screaming Santiago's name and other words in Spanish, as if crying for help. Everyone looked. There seemed to be a struggle inside the captain's office, then the porthole clapped shut.

"Maria!" Santiago shouted, and jumped out of the lifeboat.

The Chief pinched the bridge of his nose and shook his head in disgust. "Damn, Benson," he muttered. "You had one stinking job."

"Chief, what is happening? Why is Maria here?" Santiago demanded.

"Calm down, Santiago. That's an order."

"No!" he turned to the kid. "Jack Smith, where is Old Man?" He ran to him and grabbed him by the coat. "Where is Old Man, Jack Smith?"

The kid looked desperately at the Chief, who shrugged. "Go ahead," he said. "Tell Santiago what happened to the Old Man. Hell, may as well tell everyone."

"He... he drowned," the kid said. "He... he fell off the dock and drowned."

Santiago shoved him to the deck. "You lie," he snarled. He pointed at the Chief. "You turn ship around. You take Maria back to America. Now!"

"Stand down, Mr. Santiago."

Santiago yelled, "Maria!" As he pushed through the crowd to go to her, the Chief nodded at Randolph, who pulled a blackjack out of his back pocket and struck him on the back of the head. Santiago collapsed and

Randolph and another crewman jumped on him, pulled his arms behind his back and handcuffed him.

The men in the crowd began to yell, "Hey, what the hell's going on?... What'd you hit him for?... Where's the Old Man?... Hey, what the hell is this, a mutiny?... Chief, what's going on?"

The Chief calmly pulled a revolver from his waistband, pointed it in the air and fired. The report made everyone jerk. "Now hear this," he said. "The Old Man is dead. He's gone. He had an accident. There's no use getting all riled about it. As per the union contract and Coast Guard regulations, I succeed him as captain. The chief mate does not yet have his master's license, and I do. I know it's hard for some of you to understand, but there is a vanishingly small number of us in the merchant marine who are master mariners. I am one. So get used to it.

"As for the person Santiago calls Maria, well, you may recall how she got here in the first place. She was a stowaway on our last voyage from Tangier to the States. With the assistance of Mr. Santiago, I might add. And in violation of Moroccan law, the international law of the sea, and American law. The Old Man decided to give his imprimatur to this abject lawbreaking, and he allowed her to ride the rest of the way to the States as his honored guest. Again, in violation of all the laws and treaties in effect, as well as union and shipping company rules. He promised her he would help her get asylum in America. He failed.

"The government has denied her asylum, has denied her refugee status, and has in fact given us the job of returning her to her home country. That's right, we are on a contract with the United States Department of State. They are very interested in maintaining good relations with the sultan in a very complex geopolitical climate, not that any of you grease monkeys and deck apes would understand what the hell I'm talking about.

"And by the way, her real name is not Maria, it's Aisha. She's not a Spaniard, she's an Arab. She's not poor, she's privileged. She's not a refugee, she's a runaway. And if any of you have a problem with our mission, take it up with the federal government, the union, and the shipping company, because they're calling the shots. In fact, if you do anything to interfere with this mission, you will be prosecuted under federal law and drummed out of the union. You will not work in this industry ever again. So settle down, do your jobs, and let's get this over with."

Santiago was beginning to groan and stir. "What do you want us to do with him, Chief?" Randolph said.

"Take him to the brig," the Chief said. "Lock him up. And the rest of you... stay away from him."

6. Hope

THE KID KNOCKED ON THE RADIO OFFICER'S DOOR, and when it opened he smelled the peculiar odor of hot electrical circuits mixed with cigarette smoke, body odor and cheap cologne, and he heard the subtle buzzing of the communications equipment. The room was small, and the radio officer, a thin, bespectacled, bald man, sat at a table with a black telegraph key in front of him. With slender fingers he tapped a succession of dits and dahs with a speed that amazed the kid.

The Chief stood, holding the door open. "Well?" he said.

"She still won't eat," the kid said. "Everything we give her she just knocks on the floor. We can't even give her a fork because she tried to jab it into her wrist. That was after she tried to stab Benson with it. Sir."

The Chief sighed and drummed his fingers on the door jamb. "Let's see, what time is it... Twenty-one hundred hours. She hasn't eaten at all since yesterday. Is she drinking water?" he said.

"No, sir."

"Damn that bitch," he said. "She's trying to kill herself before we reach Tangier, Sparks. What the hell are we going to do?... I wonder if we could rig up a feeding tube. Hmm. Let's see, we've got plastic tubing... I suppose we could rig up some kind of plunger, maybe use a grease gun..."

"Good luck getting it past her teeth," Sparks said. His voice was high and nasal, and a cigarette wiggled in his lips as he spoke. "She already bit a chunk out of Benson."

"You're right," the Chief said. "I'd have to build some kind of wedge or clamp to hold her mouth open."

"And a frame to hold her still so she couldn't jerk her head around," Sparks offered.

"She'd wind up with bruises," the Chief said. "The sultan would be pissed. Damn. So what are we going to do, Sparks?"

"I guess there's not an engineering solution to every problem," Sparks said.

"The hell there's not," he said. "We just need tools and time. Let's see, we've got some syringes in the medical cabinet. But nothing we can use for anesthesia. Hey, what about toadstool-in-wormwood?"

"I don't know, Chief," Sparks said. "Sounds risky. Especially for the baby."

"Hell with the baby. By the time it's born we'll be long gone lonesome George. It could be born with flippers and a blowhole for all I care."

Sparks looked at him. "That baby could be born any day, Chief. Besides, that stuff could make her go into labor early. Hell, there's no telling what it could do to mother or baby. It's a real risk, Chief."

"Well, what if we took out the toadstool? Just use the absinthe?"

"You'll have to ask Apache Jack," Sparks said. "I think he mixes the stuff ashore. I doubt you could separate them once they're mixed."

All this talk of forcing the girl to eat was making the kid sweat. He felt like he was being roped into a murder plot. "Can't we just try to convince her to eat, you know, voluntarily?" he said. "Maybe give her something?"

"And what do you propose to do differently than we've been doing up to now, cabin boy?" the Chief said. "What can we give her?"

The kid had spotted something on the far side of the table from where Sparks was working the telegraph key—nearly hidden behind a cup full of sharpened pencils. It was a tiny, ceramic manger scene, very much like one his mother had, and it seemed so out-of-place among all the radio equipment.

"Hope," he said.

"Hope," the Chief said. He turned to Sparks. "See, this is the kind of crap you get from people with no technical training or aptitude."

Sparks pulled on his chin as he stared at the kid. "I don't know, Chief," he said. "The cabin boy may have a point."

"All right, tell me, cabin boy," the Chief said. "Tell me how we can persuade that stubborn, hot-headed bitch who would rather kill herself and her own child than go back to the sultan, tell me how we can give her the kind of hope you're talking about, because I know mechanics, chemistry, thermodynamics, electricity. I don't know, nor do I believe in, hope, faith, charity, or any other cockeyed magical thinking."

"I don't know," he said. "I just think she has to believe she's not, you know, going to her doom. That she's got a chance to... I don't know, maybe escape or something."

The radio officer swiveled back and forth in his chair, thinking. "Right. Somebody has to convince her she's going to be rescued. Somebody she trusts. Not us—she already thinks we're the enemy. There's only one person on the ship she'll believe, right? Santiago. She has to believe that Santiago has a plan to rescue her."

"Santiago can't even rescue himself!" The Chief laughed. "Talk about irony! You know who built that brig, don't you? Santiago. I had him build it so nobody could escape from it. Just in case we needed it. Now he's stuck in his own creation, a victim of his own superior welding and machining skills. What a dupe."

"Then somebody has to rescue Santiago," Sparks said.

The Chief shook his head in disgust. "I can't believe what I'm hearing. You're saying one of us can go free Santiago from the brig and ask him nicely to convince the girl to eat so he can rescue her when the time is right. Absurd. Santiago's not an educated man but he's no fool either. He'd sniff out what we were up to. He's not about to help us get that girl back to the sultan. He's as stubborn as she is. And he doesn't trust us."

"I'm not talking about one of us, Chief."

"Well then, who? Who can do it, Sparks? Who can carry out this ridiculous scheme of yours?"

"The cabin boy." The radio officer had not taken his eyes off the kid.

"The cabin boy! The cabin boy and whose army?" he laughed.

"The cabin boy and the Old Man," Sparks said.

The Chief spoke through gritting teeth. "I told you I don't want to hear his name again. Besides, in case you missed it, he's dead."

"Bear with me, Chief. Remember, it wasn't just Santiago she trusted. It was the Old Man too. She worships the guy. Calls him Santo Viejo, or something like that."

"So you're suggesting she pray to her beloved, but still dead, saint for intercession? I'm not following you."

"What if the Old Man is still alive?"

The Chief stared at him.

"Look, the only reason any of us have for believing the Old Man is dead is... the cabin boy, right?"

"Nah, I sent the other two out there. They saw the evidence."

"They didn't see his body. Chief, the Old Man jumped into Boston harbor in February a few years back, in nothing but his underwear. Just for the hell of it. Cold as hell. He actually had to bust a hole in the ice. Remember?"

The Chief scratched his chin. "Yeah. He called it the Boston ice tea party. We all thought he was a fool."

"Remember who was there, Chief? Watching him? Cheering him on?"

"Yeah, yeah, yeah, Santiago. So what's your point, Sparks, that he was just playing a practical joke on the kid last night? That he's not really dead?"

"No, but that's something Santiago could believe. If the Old Man was just warmed up on peppermint schnapps, as usual, he could have jumped in to play a joke on the kid, then climbed back out. But it wasn't just schnapps, was it?"

"Nah. Toadstool-in-wormwood. Cabin boy, where'd you say he thought he was?"

"Tahiti, sir."

"Tahiti. Yeah, the Old Man liked Tahiti. Toadstool-in-wormwood will take a man anywhere he wants to go, Sparks. In this case it took him on a detour to the bottom of the bay. He's dead, for sure."

"Chief," the radio officer said, "the point is, Santiago doesn't know you spiked the Old Man's schnapps. He could be made to believe that the Old Man's still alive. Tell him the Old Man just jumped in to play a joke on the kid, but before he could even towel off, you grabbed the kid and the girl and got on the ship and hightailed it back to sea, destination Tangier, to collect the sultan's reward. Tell Santiago the Old Man's bound and determined to get his ship back, and to rescue the girl. Tell him the Old Man's got a plan to fly to Tangier, and to meet the ship on the pilot boat. You know, take back his ship, sail back to the States, not even go to the dock in Tangier. But the girl has to stay alive and healthy, you know, I mean she can't die before the Old Man has a chance to rescue her, can she? Look, if Santiago tells her this, she'll believe it. And she'll eat."

"And who tells Santiago?"

"Like I said, the cabin boy."

"Sparks, come on, this is idiotic. And why would Santiago believe this little squirt? How could the cabin boy come by all this information about the Old Man?"

"This is where I volunteer my services, Chief. The cabin boy tells Santiago, look, Sparks knows the Old Man's alive. In fact, Sparks has been communicating with the Old Man by radio. And Sparks, he's on the Old Man's side, and..."

"Are you?"

"The Old Man's dead, Chief," he said. "You're the captain now."

"Remember that."

"All right, so the kid tells Santiago that Sparks is secretly working with the Old Man on this rescue plan, and the plan's really simple: just get the girl to start eating again, and then everybody just sit tight 'til we get to Tangier. The Old Man shows up and saves the day. Done deal. Nobody really has to do anything, except Santiago has to get the girl to start eating again. And so the kid tells Santiago that Sparks stole the brig key from the Chief and gave it to him so he could let Santiago out..."

"So if you're the leader of the disloyal opposition, why don't you just go down there and tell him yourself, Sparks? Just take the key and let him out?"

"Because I'm a coward.   Everybody including Santiago knows that. He knows I'd never take a chance getting caught with the key. He'd think you put me up to it."

"OK, so why wouldn't he think the same thing of the cabin boy?"

"Because the kid considers himself a prisoner too, Chief, and he wants to escape too. He just tells Santiago you shanghaied him…"

"Hell with that, I got his John Hancock on a contract, in his own hand."

"Yeah, you know that and I know that, Chief, but Santiago doesn't know that. So the kid tells Santiago, look, the Chief kidnapped me and I'm afraid he's going to kill me or sell me for a slave in Tangier or something. I overheard him talking, and that's what he's planning to do. I need to get out with you guys."

"Transparent trickery," the Chief said. "I wouldn't fall for it."

"Santiago's not you," the radio officer said. "He's not a thinker. He's a believer. He wants to believe."

"In what?"

"Hope."

The Chief shook his head with a disgusted sneer. "All this fantastical hoopla just to get a teenage girl to eat. And a pregnant one at that! Hell, all the pregnant women I've ever known have eaten like pigs. You couldn't keep them out of the slop chest if you tried." He studied the kid for a while, pondering. "All right, what the hell," he said, fishing into his pocket, "give it a shot."

He handed the brig key to Sparks and looked back at the kid. "What's your name, cabin boy?"

"Jack Smith, sir."

"Good. You've been listening. You know the script. You go down to the brig, tell Santiago the plan. Keep it simple. If he buys it, let him out. Tell him I'm on the bridge, and to sneak up and tap on the porthole of my office. Little Suzie Q will open it. He'll convince her to eat, and then he'll go back to his hole and you'll lock him up again. And then everybody just waits for the Old Man to come on the pilot boat in Tangier and save the day. Got it?"

"Yes, sir."

"And if this plan doesn't work, we'll go to Plan B, which is to shoot Santiago for a mutineer, sell the cabin boy's marbled rump roast in the market in Tangier, and force feed the girl like a goose being fattened for pâté before returning her to the sultan for the princely recompense he has offered. Do I make myself clear?"

"Yes, sir."

"Good. Give him the key, Sparks." The Chief turned to walk out the door, grumbling about "a lot of psycho-bunk and overly complicated foolishness... elegant simplicity is the hallmark of good design."

The radio officer handed the key to the cabin boy, but held onto it firmly as the kid grasped it. When the kid looked at him, Sparks gave him an almost imperceptible nod before releasing the key.

7. The Guitar Lesson

DESIGNED BY THE CHIEF AND BUILT BY SANTIAGO, the brig was a masterpiece of elegant simplicity. It was situated in the engine room near the day engineer's tool shop where the light was dim and the noise and heat unrelenting. The Chief boasted that the bars could not be cut or torched open, nor could the lock be picked—at least without sounding alarms—and yet as the cabin boy approached he saw a man squatting in front of its door wiggling a thin strip of metal in the keyhole.

Santiago was sitting on the deck of the brig with his back against the bulkhead, playing a guitar. For a moment, the cabin boy was mesmerized by the music. Santiago played with a natural grace and power and without the slightest hint of self-consciousness; he played the way Chick Charles always wanted to play. And as he played he sang, or it sounded like singing, but the cabin boy realized that Santiago was speaking in a lilting, soothing voice, trying to calm the lock-picker as the man struggled with his delicate task.

"Take your time, Wiper Billy Sunday, take your time... Forgive tumblers, for they know not what they do... They are little children, love them, preacher man, be easy and love them like your Lord Jesus loves the little children... Breathe deep, breathe easy, Wiper Billy Sunday, let your heart beat slow... the heat is your friend, my friend, your suffering is holy, like Jesus on the cross... forgive tumblers, for they know not what they do..."

The wiper groaned and flopped backward, panting and wiping the sweat from his eyes with his sleeve. "I can't do it, Santiago, I just ain't cut out for this sorta thing."

Santiago stopped playing. "Hey Wiper Billy Sunday, look here. We have visitor. Hey Jack Smith, why you here? You already bring my supper. I no am hungry now."

The cabin boy looked at the man called Wiper Billy Sunday. He was built like a scarecrow, tall and sinewy, with huge clumsy hands, large facial features and a voice that sounded like it was rumbling out of a deep well. He was an unskilled broom pusher and rag wiper, thus the job title, and a lay preacher for any crewman who would listen to his sermons, but despite this lowly position the cabin boy didn't want to talk to Santiago with the wiper present.

But before he could say anything about it, the wiper sat up and said to him, "Hey, young fella, you got delicate hands, can you help me open this lock?"

"Uhhh..."

"Come on, Jack Smith, we need to get him out. Scuttlebutt from topside is that Maria won't eat nothing, and she won't drink nothing either, and she's liable to die of thirst and starvation if she don't eat or drink. And she could lose the baby, son, and that'd be a pluperfect shame, dad-gummit, a pluperfect shame. That gal's stubborn as a mule, lemme tellya, stubborn as a gol-dang mule, and she's dead set against goin' back to that sultan in Tangier, she don't want to be nobody's concubine no more, see, she was kidnapped from Spain some years back on account of how beautiful she was, even as a child, it just ain't right, Jack Smith, people treatin' people thataway! But look, the Old Man ain't dead like you thought, he's alive, I'll confess that truth on a stack of Bibles, and he's coming back, sure as we're standing here. But Maria, she's gotta stay alive 'til then, can't you see what I'm talking about? She's got to stay alive 'til the Old Man comes, and the onliest one she'll listen to is Santiago here. So you got to help me get him out, so we can sneak him up 'ar and he can tell her what's what and get her to eat. Whaddya say, son? Will you help me?"

The cabin boy stood there, stunned and wordless.

Santiago laughed. "Hey Jack Smith. You know how to pick lock?"

"Uhhh..."

"Come on Jack Smith," Wiper Billy Sunday said, "have a heart, son. Won't you help us? You don't want Maria and her baby to die, do you?"

The cabin boy scratched his head. The whole way down to the brig he had worried that Santiago would see through his "transparent trickery," as the Chief called it, and he'd be stubborn and refuse him, and then the Chief would turn to Plan B, and then it would be rump roast or stumps for the cabin boy. And he imagined each option in gruesome detail and he was close to deciding he'd rather be rump roast because at least then he'd have his hands and could possibly escape, because for some reason getting his hands chopped off seemed like the most horrible thing that could possibly happen to him. But now everything was seemingly just falling into his lap, and it was just too easy, and he didn't trust it. And he thought of how Sparks gave him that strange, secret little nod as he handed him the brig key, but he still couldn't figure out what it meant.

Santiago gave a flamenco strum on his guitar. "You like guitar, Jack Smith? You help us, I give you my guitar. I give you lesson too, yes? But first I teach you to pick lock. The wiper, he has no good hands. But you, I see you have very good hands. You have hands can do great things. Great things, Jack Smith."

The cabin boy looked at one man, then the other. He said, "OK, I'll help, but... you have to promise, after you tell Maria to eat, you have to come back here and get in the brig again, and, and you have to stay there 'til the Old Man comes, OK? I mean, I'll help you... if you do that."

"Yeah, sure, Jack Smith, sure," Santiago said. "Is good plan."

Wiper Billy Sunday squeezed the cabin boy's shoulder in one powerful hand as he stuck the lock pick between his teeth like a toothpick and pulled a little Bible out of his pocket. "Son," he said, the lock pick bobbing as he spoke, "I do so swear on the holiest of holy books, on the gospel of Christ Jesus himself, that ol' Santiago will do right by you, and he won't hurt or betray you none, so help me God, Amen." Then he pinched the lock pick between his massive thumb and forefinger and held it toward the kid.

The cabin boy sighed nervously and said, "I don't need that." He reached into his pocket and pulled out the key.

"Where you get key?" Santiago said.

Here's where the resistance comes, he thought. He steeled himself for it and recited his line. "Umm... The radio officer, what's-his-name, Sparks gave it to me. He, uhh, he stole it from the Chief. He..."

"Sparks!" Wiper Billy Sunday said. "I told you, Santiago! Sparks is one of us! He was saved last trip. He accepted Jesus when he saw how the Old Man treated Maria. He come to me and he said he's seen grace, and he confessed his sins and was saved. I knew it! Praise the Lord! I just knew it!"

"Yah, Sparks good man, good man," Santiago said. "OK, Jack Smith, is time."

The cabin boy took a deep breath, then stuck the key in the lock and opened it. Santiago pushed open the door and stepped out of the brig. He patted the cabin boy on the shoulder and said, "Good boy, Jack Smith, good boy. No! No, no good boy... Good man! Good man, Jack Smith. You are man tonight."

Santiago reached into his pocket, pulled out two little bottles and handed one to the wiper, who looked at the handwritten label and grinned. "Toadstool-in-wormwood. What you got on your mind, Santiago?"

"You take, put in coffee for engineer, is eight-to-twelve watch, so is O'Leary. Tell him is Irish coffee and merry Christmas from you. O'Leary like Irish coffee. Me and Jack Smith, we go up to captain's office. When O'Leary go, you know, crazy, you shut main throttle, stop ship. When bridge calls, you no answer. Chief come running down below, see what problem is, like always. And me and Jack Smith, we get Maria. And then we go to lifeboat, lower lifeboat, and we go. We go meet Old Man."

"Wait a minute!" the cabin boy said. "That's not the plan! We have to wait 'til we get to Tangier. That's where the Old Man..."

"The plan change," Santiago said. "Old Man no wait for Tangier. We no wait for Tangier. Old Man come tonight! Tonight!"

"But... wait... you promised!"

Santiago ran into the tool shop and retrieved a large canvas sack. He came out and thrust it at the cabin boy. "Take, Jack Smith. Go to galley. Put food in for Maria. Then, you go to lifeboat number one. You remember this morning? Same one. I get Maria. I meet you there."

"No, wait... this... this isn't possible! No, look, Santiago... It's freezing out there! And... and it's really, really windy! And sleet and... We can't put Maria in a lifeboat out there! It's suicide..."

"Maria is strong, Jack Smith. I am great lifeboat captain! Great lifeboat captain! Is OK. We no be in lifeboat long time. Old Man come soon tonight, find us."

"No, look, Santiago, we can't..."

Santiago gave the cabin boy a little shove. "Go now, go to galley."

"No, Santiago! Look, the Old Man is dead, OK? He's dead, I saw him fall into the water and drown. And... and I heard the Chief say he spiked the Old Man's schnapps with... with that stuff you've got, toadstool-whatever. He's not coming, Santiago! You have to figure out a different way!"

But Santiago wasn't listening. He had run back into the workshop and was gathering tools in a small sack.

"Oh ye of little faith," Wiper Billy Sunday said to the cabin boy. "Son, ain't no little cold bath could kill the Old Man! He's a reg'lar walrus, ain't that right, Santiago? Six-and-a-half feet of blubber and beard! You remember when we saw him jump in Boston harbor that day, Santiago? Well hell, I just about forgot, you jumped in with him, didn't you, Santiago? A couple a crazy sea lions, is what! It was a lot colder than it is now. I declare I never saw such a splash as when that three-hunnerd pound sonofagun hit the water! Your splash weren't near as big, Santiago."

The cabin boy's mind stammered, then spun around. "But it's... But... Wait, what did you just say?"

"Biggest splash I ever saw," the wiper said. "And in the coldest water."

"Wait. The Old Man... was three hundred pounds?"

"And six-and-a-half foot if he was an inch! I thought you said you saw him. He gave you his coat, didn't he?"

"Yeah, but he was... the guy I saw was... kinda scrawny. But... he was wearing the coat and hat. The sleeves were... rolled up... He..."

"Oh, Lordy!" Wiper Billy Sunday said. "Well, don't you see? It's clear as day! The Old Man just met some bum on the street, gave him his coat and hat, you know, he's always helping out the poor man, the widow, the orphan. And he likely gave the poor guy his schnapps, too, not knowing the Chief done spiked it! You didn't meet the Old Man, Jack Smith, you met the vagrant, see? And he only gave you his coat and hat because he was flyin' high on the toadstool-in-wormwood! Hell, the poor guy probably thought he was in Hawiya or someplace. Don't you suppose it's so, Santiago?"

Santiago finished putting some items into a small sack and tying it to his belt. "Yes, Wiper Billy Sunday. Is true," he said. "I know Old Man. He will hire boat. Or buy one, or steal one. Fast boat. He come after us. We look for running lights. Also there is flare in lifeboat. We use so he can find us. OK, Wiper Billy Sunday, you go give O'Leary spiked coffee. Jack Smith, you go get food from galley for Maria. Meet me at lifeboat number one, ten minutes. I go get Maria."

"But wait, please!" the cabin boy said. "I mean, have you been outside? The weather's terrible. It's freezing cold, and... I mean, it's bad enough being on a ship, but in a lifeboat? That's crazy! Can't we just... Can't we just help him aboard when he gets here? I mean, instead of..."

"No, Jack Smith. Chief has guns. Chief and his men shoot Old Man, bang-bang, easy. No good, Jack Smith, no good."

"OK, but... Come on, seriously, why would he come tonight? Why tonight? It doesn't make any sense!"

"Because," Santiago said with a grin, "Is Christmas Eve. Old Man come, Jack Smith. Tonight. Have faith."

"Hold on, brothers," Wiper Billy Sunday said. He placed his giant hands on the shoulders of Santiago and the cabin boy, and bowed his head. "Heavenly Father, we ask you to receive the soul of the old vagrant what gave his coat to Jack here into your loving embrace, may he rest in peace. And we ask you to watch over Santiago and Maria and Jack and keep them safe 'til the Old Man finds them, if that is your will. Forgive us our sins. In Jesus' name we pray, Amen."

8. Lower Away

AT FIRST THE CABIN BOY DIDN'T KNOW WHAT TO DO, so he stood there for a minute after Santiago and Wiper Billy Sunday left the brig. Then he went to the galley and got food for Maria. He figured he had to do that anyway, since that was the job the Chief gave him, and he put some in the canvas sack Santiago gave him for the lifeboat, and some in a cardboard box to take to the captain's office, as he had done earlier in the day. If Santiago succeeded in freeing Maria and fleeing in the lifeboat, well then, she'd have something to eat on the boat before drowning or freezing to death. If Santiago got shot, which he figured was a good deal more likely, then a sack of food on the lifeboat wouldn't hurt anybody and he would have done all he could do.

As he stepped out into the frigid night and made his way to the lifeboat, all he knew was, he wasn't about to lower away in that lifeboat with Santiago. That'd be suicide, pure and simple. The ship rolled and bucked on the angry sea, and the deck and railings were slick with gathering ice. As he slid the sack of food under the canvas cover he felt the sting of the ice needles in the wind on his face and hands, and he remembered how close he came to freezing to death on the street before the Old Man—or the old vagrant, whichever it was—gave him the pea coat and hat he was wearing.

And he didn't want to be anywhere near the captain's office while Santiago made his attempt to rescue Maria. The Chief was armed, as were at least five or six of the men who were working with him, and if Santiago stepped one foot from the agreed-upon plan, the cabin boy figured the likeliest outcome would be just what the Chief had promised before: Santiago would get shot and they would "engineer" a way to force food and water into Maria until they reached Tangier.

But it was the other part of "Plan B" that was worrying him. How did the Chief put it? The stumpy cabin boy's rump roast would be sold in the market in Tangier. The kid had a vivid imagination to start with, and standing out there by the lifeboat waiting for something to happen, his mind churned up one horrible depredation after another that could befall him in such a distant, dusty, godforsaken place.

And so he tried to shake his head free of those images, and forced himself to think of what he could say to persuade the Chief to have mercy on him and send him home. He shoved his hands deep in the pockets of his pea coat and stomped his feet to keep warm while he tried out one scripted line after another.

"Chief, he promised he'd go along with the plan, but then when he got out he just changed his mind, I swear... Look, I think I can get her to eat, I really do... I mean, that's what you want, right? To get her to eat so she'll be alive when we get to Tangier... I mean, maybe Santiago's not the only one who can convince her to eat... I might be able to do it, just let me try... Ah, hell, I don't speak Spanish, who am I kidding?... Or, you could just give her some of that, what'd they call it, toadstool-in-wormwood, and she might just eat on her own, right? I mean, so what if it hurts the baby?... Dammit, I don't want to hurt the baby... Aw, hell..."

Suddenly, the sounds of the ship's gargantuan engines died down and the cabin boy felt the vessel lose its forward momentum as Wiper Billy Sunday closed the throttle down below. It was eerily quiet for a minute and then, just as Santiago had predicted, the Chief left the bridge and ran down to the engine room.

Sooner than the cabin boy ever thought possible, Santiago emerged from the midships house and, with his arms around her to steady her from the rolling of the ship, guided Maria to the lifeboat. Moving fast, and with the skill of an acrobat, Santiago jumped onto the lifeboat, removed the cover and tossed it aside. Then he picked Maria up in his arms and lifted her into the boat.

"Jack Smith!" he hissed. "Come, we go now!"

The cabin boy backed away from him, shaking his head. "I'm sorry, Santiago... I... I put the bag of food in the boat, but... I can't go with you..." He turned to walk away, but a shock went through him as someone grabbed his arm from behind.

"You best get on that lifeboat," a high, nasal voice said. "It's your only chance."

"Sparks?" the cabin boy said. "But..."

"The Chief's never going to let you go home," the radio officer said. "You know too much. Hell, he never was going to let you go home anyway. It was never part of his plan. Let me tell you something, kid. Whatever it is you've been thinking, about what could happen to you in Tangier, well that's not even close to the hell you're gonna find yourself in if you stay on this ship. Trust me. I've seen it before. The Chief, he's an evil man. The devil incarnate. The things he told you about Tangier, they're not idle threats. Get in that lifeboat. Go with Santiago. Help him save that girl and her baby. It's your only chance." He pushed the cabin boy toward the boat. Santiago reached out, grabbed him by the lapels of his pea coat, and pulled him aboard.

"OK, Sparks," Santiago said. "Lower away! And God bless you, my friend!" The radio officer took the controls and the lifeboat descended on its cables from the gravity davit, down through the slicing night wind to the mysterious sea.

9. Shots in the Dark

THE CABIN BOY FEARED THE ESCAPE PARTY would not even make it to the water in one piece, much less back to dry land. With every gust of wind and every roll and pitch of the ship, the lifeboat would swing and bang against the hull such that he feared it would crack open like an egg and spill them all out to drown.

But Santiago was a master of his craft, and fearless, and he used his hands and body and voice to steady the lifeboat and its passengers in their descent. Santiago handed a flashlight to the cabin boy and told him to shine it down on the water so that he could see when to release the boat from its grips.

The sight made the kid dizzy with terror. As the ship rolled and the swells passed underneath, it felt as if the lifeboat was a yo-yo in the hands of a petulant, childish god, slapping the surface of the water before being yanked up again. Santiago would have to make the release at exactly the right moment or the little boat would fall through the void and capsize when it hit the water.

"More aft! More aft!" Santiago yelled, urging the cabin boy to move the beam of the flashlight, but the kid was unused to nautical directions and he jerked the light erratically. "No! No! Aft, Jack Smith! Aft!" The kid shifted toward the seaward side of the boat for a better position, and as he did a wave slapped his hand and he dropped the flashlight into the sea.

The light spun and wiggled as it sank into the deep and the cabin boy yelled out, "Oh my God! I dropped it! I'm sorry, I'm sorry..."

But Santiago released the boat at that moment and it smacked into the water with a violent impact and a roll that nearly sent the cabin boy overboard.

"Ha ha!" Santiago cheered as he crabbed quickly toward the lifeboat's engine. "You hold Maria," he said and slapped him on the back. "I start engine. Go! Go, Jack Smith!"

The kid crawled, more like a newborn kitten than a crab, to where Maria was sitting. He sat next to her, but he didn't know what to do. "Jack Smith!" she cried, and clutched the Old Man's pea coat. The cabin boy spread his feet wide for balance, then put one arm around her and with the other gripped the seat.

The little engine sputtered and coughed and then rumbled to life. Santiago began to talk, in Spanish to Maria, and in his broken English to the cabin boy, back and forth, urging them to be calm and have faith, everything would be all right. His voice was strong and steady, even cheerful.

The cabin boy was not a swimmer. But even if I could swim, he thought, what good would it do? The distance to shore, the depth of the water, the paralyzing cold, all may as well have been infinite for all the good swimming would do. He looked at the ship, and his anxiety to get back aboard was reeling into a panic. But there was no way to get back up. Sparks was retracting the lifeboat cables and there was no ladder, no handholds, nothing but the smooth sides of the hull. An image from a long past Sunday school class flashed through his mind: all those people left outside the ark, swimming in the raging floodwaters, vainly pounding on the gopherwood hull, begging Noah to let them in, and being denied salvation.

And here they were—these three who only a minute ago were passengers aboard that ark and able to stay there, safe and sound if not free—intentionally leaving it to brave the murderous sea, if "brave" is the right word for such foolishness. The only thing keeping the cabin boy from diving into the water and pounding on the side of the ship like some damned soul at the ark was Santiago.

The Spaniard was a solid rock of self-confidence, and the cabin boy locked his eyes and his hopes on him as the day engineer steered the puttering little boat away from the ship and into that dark night.

And then a spotlight shined down from the lifeboat deck toward the water. For a few seconds it swept this way and that until it found the lifeboat. A voice yelled through the wind: "There they are!" Like a stage performer, Santiago stood and faced the light. "Hey Chief!" he yelled. "Have a good time in Tangier! Sorry we could not go with you! Bon voyage!" And with a grin he kissed his fingertips, threw his arms out to the sides and laughed.

Next to the spotlight there was a smaller, sudden flash of light and a loud crack, and sparks flew as a bullet ricocheted off the engine. The chugging of the diesel died and the lifeboat stopped moving.

"You god-damned son of a bitch, Chief!" Santiago yelled. He bent over the engine to try to restart it. Another gunshot rang out. "You no stop us, you son of a whore!" he yelled. He pulled the oars from their racks and set them in the oarlocks. "You get in front of Maria, Jack Smith," he said. "Protect from bullets. I row. I fix engine when we get out of... how you say? Out of range."

The cabin boy didn't think about it. Santiago told him to do it, so he did it. He placed his body between Maria and the ship. "Please, God, less waves!" Santiago said as he crossed himself. Then he sat down and pulled on the oars with all his might. The kid watched him, sustained by his power and defiance and skill: the way he leaned far forward at the beginning of the stroke, the way he twisted his wrists to set the blades in the water for the best purchase, the way he pulled, first with his back and legs, and then with his shoulders and arms, never flailing, but with control and rhythm. "You watch, Jack Smith!" he called over his shoulder. "I teach you to row like a man!"

Another shot cracked the night and Santiago's body jerked backward as if an invisible fist had punched him in the chest. He groaned, sat back upright, and tried to pull on the oars again. Then he released the oars, stood on trembling legs and turned to face the cabin boy and Maria. He placed his hand on the cabin boy's shoulder. "You are... how you say? You are el remero now, my friend. You must row." He looked past them to the West. "I see light," he said. "Old Man come. Row, Jack Smith, row like man..."

The next shot spun Santiago around and hit the cabin boy square in the chest, knocking him back against Maria. Santiago stumbled over the side of the lifeboat and splashed into the water. For a brief moment—just long enough to say, "Row, Jack Smith, row!"—Santiago held onto the gunwale of the boat, then released his grip.

Maria screamed, "Santiago!" and reached for the man, but too late. The cabin boy pulled her back, then he sat in the oarsman's seat and, using the long sleeves of the Old Man's pea coat as mittens, gripped the handles of the oars and began to pull. He desperately wanted to reach under his pea coat to feel for the wound and the blood he feared were there, but he didn't feel any pain and he even more desperately wanted to pull the lifeboat out of firing range until he could think of how he could return to the ship without getting shot again.

He kept expecting some effects from the bullet he felt hit his chest, some searing pain or some dizziness from loss of blood, but no such feeling came. He turned around once to look for the light Santiago said he had seen—the Old Man's light. But all he saw was the glare of the ship's spotlight sweep the ocean just beyond the lifeboat, and in that glare for just a brief moment he saw a furious thrashing in the water, and a rope tied to the bow leading taut to the thrashing as if hooked to some enormous fish that was pulling the lifeboat away from the ship.

Santiago, he thought. Santiago is swimming the lifeboat away from the ship! What else could it be? The cabin boy recalled what Wiper Billy Sunday had said: that Santiago had jumped into the freezing Boston harbor with the Old Man, just for kicks. But this was not the harbor, this was the deep sea, it was rough and frigid and he had been shot twice—there was no way Santiago could possibly last. It was a sacrifice, for him, for Maria, for the baby. Santiago's sacrifice filled the cabin boy with a shame like fire. He couldn't let the Spaniard do it alone. He began to pull on the oars with all his might.

As he rowed he became aware that the wind was dying down. Though the long swells remained, the chop and whitecaps that made it so difficult to gain a purchase on the water with the oars diminished as the surface became smoother. From the ship the spotlight jerked down as if the operator had lost control of it for a few seconds. In the darkness, the cabin boy pulled hard, and the more he pulled, the more distance he put between the lifeboat and the ship.

The spotlight began sweeping the sea again but somehow kept missing the lifeboat. Without the howling of the wind, the cabin boy feared that Maria's sobbing would give away their position, so he hissed at her to "Shh!... be quiet, Maria! Shhhh..." and she seemed to understand.

There was a loud squeal and then a voice sounded from a bullhorn. "Cabin boy, this is your captain speaking," the Chief said. "Shine a flashlight or something, son, so we can find you and bring you back to the ship. No harm will come to you. Santiago was a mutineer, and he paid the price. It's done, son. Come on back. I guarantee you safe passage."

The cabin boy was silent for a moment, then put his hand to his mouth to respond, but Maria slapped his ear and hissed, "No!"

"Come on, boy," the Chief said. "There's a flare gun in a box there in the boat. Just pull it out and shoot off a flare so we can rescue you."

There was another squeal and some strange grunting and then another voice could be heard on the bullhorn. "No!" it said. "Keep going, cabin boy, keep going! He's going to kill you..."

Amplified by the bullhorn, the next gunshot cracked loud. The cabin boy saw the barrel flash, but it looked different this time, as if the shot was aimed aboard the ship. The Chief's voice sounded again. "Never mind Sparks," he said. "He's drunk. Now you'd better think, cabin boy. You're out on the deep sea in an open boat in the eye of a winter storm. That eye will pass in a little while. Now's the time to come back aboard, where it's nice and warm and dry..."

The cabin boy felt his chest. His finger found the bullet hole in the pea coat. He pushed his finger into the hole until he touched something hidden away in an inner pocket, something he hadn't noticed before. He pressed on it, and squeezed it through the coat. Whatever it was, he figured, it had saved his life.

"Santiago..." Maria whimpered.

The cabin boy turned around and peered into the night. For just a moment, he thought he saw a light, but it could have been a star shining through a break in the cloud cover. He began to row toward it. He pulled on the oars with long, strong strokes, exactly as he had seen Santiago do it.

10. Miracles

HE ROWED, AND THE LIGHTS OF THE SHIP GREW SMALLER and more distant. As he got tired, he slowed his pace but he kept rowing with smooth, steady strokes. The effort kept him warm, but there was something else, too. He discovered he had a knack for rowing, and it was a strangely satisfying feeling, which he gladly indulged in favor of the fatal despair that lurked all around. There was a rhythm to rowing, and he began to sing to the beat the oars made in the oarlocks, first just in his head, then in a whisper, and then as the lights of the ship grew more distant, a low, steady chant.

First, it was "Row, Row, Row Your Boat," and then "Aura Lee" and "Love Me Tender," which, of course, have the same melody, and then "Paper Moon" and "Home on the Range" and "Sixteen Tons," and all the songs from the books he had when he was teaching himself to play the guitar. And he thought again of Santiago, and how natural and easy his guitar playing was as he sat there in the brig, and then he remembered that Santiago promised to give him his guitar and teach him how to play if he would just let him out of the brig.

Was Santiago dead? Or was he still pulling on the rope? Occasionally the cabin boy would leave off a couple of strokes to see if he could feel the tug on the bow line, but he couldn't be sure of it so he would begin to pull and sing again. He didn't want to stop rowing and go check, for he was afraid of what he might find.

He was a stroke away from giving in to the temptation to check when he heard Maria making strange, rhythmic sounds, and he thought she was urging him to keep singing, maybe to chase away that lurking despair.

And so he started singing "Only You," but the noises she was making began to sound more frustrated and annoyed, so he wondered if she wanted him to shut up, or row faster, or maybe to turn the boat around and row back to the ship. He asked her, "Maria, what's wrong?" even though he knew he couldn't understand Spanish, and when she did answer, it wasn't in words anyway, it was just in more frustrated, angry grunts and groans. And as the groans became longer and more straining, he realized it wasn't his labor she was agitated about.

He stopped rowing and turned around. "Oh my God," he said. "Maria, are you having your baby?"

She answered by grabbing his collar and digging her fingernails into the skin of his neck and letting out a long, straining, squealing groan. When that contraction was over he was able to peel her fingers from his neck and blurt out, "Maria, what do I do? I don't know what to do! Oh my God!"

In the eye of the storm the clouds had parted and a bright moon shone down from directly overhead. Maria sat there with her legs spread wide, panting. "This can't be happening," the cabin boy said, veering toward panic. "Oh my God this cannot be happening! Maria, I can't... This won't happen right now, will it? I mean... this takes time, doesn't it? We... Oh my God! We have to go back to the ship! Maria..."

Suddenly Maria slapped him hard in the face as another contraction began and pointed wildly down between her legs, screaming in Spanish. She let out another long straining squeal and the cabin boy finally dared look down there. The baby was crowning. The moon was shining down through the open eye of the storm, and its light shone off the top of the baby's slimy head as steam rose from it. The contraction eased. As the next one started, Maria grabbed the cabin boy's wrists and shoved his hands down into a catching position. He could not believe how fast it was all happening. He whined a long, high-pitched but very unmusical whine as he saw the baby's head come out, face up. He cradled the head in his right hand and soon the rest of the body followed. He caught its bottom in his other hand, but it was so slimy that it started to slip out of his grasp and as he jerked to catch it, his hand slapped its bottom and the baby coughed and then started to cry.

Maria sounded like she was sobbing and laughing and panting all at once. She opened her coat, and then the top of her dress and motioned for him to lay the baby on her bare skin. He did. Then he stood there, looking down on her in the moonlight. "Maria," he said, "we should go back to the ship. Let me take you back." He knew she didn't understand, so he pointed in that direction.

"No, Jack Smith, no," she said. She jerked her thumb in the direction they had been rowing away from the ship. "Santo Viejo," she said. "Old Man..."

He turned to look toward the ship. From that direction he thought he could hear a puttering noise like the sound of the lifeboat engine, and then the bullhorn again, but he couldn't tell what was being said. Then he heard the crack of a gunshot. "They're coming," he said.

The baby changed everything. He didn't know if it was a boy or a girl. All he knew was: it was alive. He looked down at Maria again and he knew as he had never known anything in his life that he had to get her and that newborn child to safety.

He would follow Santiago. He would go to the Old Man.

The eye was passing over. The moon went behind the clouds. The wind was starting up again. He could feel the sting of sleet on his face. He took off the Old Man's sea captain hat and placed it on Maria's head. He pulled the chin strap over the bill and cinched it under her chin. Then he took off the Old Man's pea coat and laid it as a blanket over mother and child.

I am not the cabin boy, he told himself. I am the oarsman. Then he sat down, gripped the oar handles in his bare hands, and began to row. With icy needles of sleet stinging his head and face and hands, and the chill wind piercing his thin shirt, he began to sing "Here Comes Santa Claus" to the beat of his oars on the water.

11. St. Brendan's Hospital

"WELL, WELL, LOOK WHO'S WAKING UP," she said.

He opened his eyes to see a woman in a white nurse's hat and uniform looking down at him. He was lying on his back. His head felt fuzzy and his mouth was dry. He smacked his lips.

"Thirsty?" she said. "Here." She placed the straw between his lips and he drank water from the glass she was holding. "So, how are we feeling this morning? I hear you had quite a night last night."

"Where am I?" he said.

"You're in Saint Brendan's Hospital. I'm Nurse Landers, and I'll be taking care of you this morning."

"How did I get here? Wait... Where's Maria? Is she OK?"

"Maria's fine," the nurse said. "The baby's fine, too. Thanks to you, I'm told. Do you remember anything about what happened last night?"

"Maria had her baby," he said. "And I rowed, and... I went as long as I could, and... I guess I don't remember. Maybe I passed out. It was cold."

"That's saying the least of it," the nurse said. "The man who brought you here said when he found you, you were pretty delirious. You were singing, and talking about all kinds of things, and..." She placed the back of her fingers against his forehead. "And you were pretty much covered in ice. He said your hands... were frozen to the oars. Do you remember that?"

He thought for a while. "I think so. I remember I was glad for the ice."

"Glad for it? Why?"

"I couldn't have kept my grip on the oars otherwise," he said. "Once my hands got coated in the ice I couldn't let go. So I could keep rowing. I had to keep rowing. To get to the Old Man."

"The Old Man? You mean the one who brought you in here? Big guy, white beard?"

He stared at her. "He found me?"

"Yes. He said you must have rowed for hours. He said had you not rowed as far as you did, he never would have found you, and you and Maria and the baby would all have died out there. My God, I can't imagine being out in a lifeboat in weather like that! He tried to pry your hands from the oars, but... he couldn't. So he had to chop you free with an axe. When he brought you in here you were still gripping the oar handles in your hands."

He lay quiet. "So," the nurse said, "How do you know the Old Man?"

"I don't," he said.

"Well, he seems to know you. We wouldn't have known your name if he hadn't told us. That's how we were able to contact your parents. They gave us permission to go ahead with the procedure. They're in talking to the surgeon now. Do you want me to go get them?"

He was about to say, "What procedure?" but was interrupted by a knock on the door and a familiar voice saying, "Can I come in?"

He turned to look. "Celeste?" he said. "What are you... How did you know I was here?"

She hesitated, then stepped into the room. "Hi, Chick," she said. "I... I didn't know what happened the other night... when you left the party. Somebody told me you were here."

"Don't tell me, let me guess," the nurse said. "Tall, heavyset guy, white beard."

"I... I don't know about that," Celeste said. "He called me on the phone. He said you were in the hospital and I should come and see you. That it was important. I asked him who he was. He just said he was the Old Man. He didn't tell me a name. He said you told him you left your guitar at the party, Chick. He asked me to bring it, so... here." She had been carrying the guitar by the neck. She held it toward him.

When he raised his arms to receive it, a look of horror swept across her face and she dropped the guitar on the ground and held her hands over her mouth. "Oh, Chick," she breathed, and stepped backward. She blinked, and tears ran down her cheeks.

His forearms were wrapped in thick white bandages, which made them look like cotton swabs. He stared at them for the first time since he awoke, and wrinkled his brow as if something was amiss and he couldn't quite put his finger on what it was. He tapped his forearms together like sticks and winced in pain.

"Easy, now," the nurse said.

"What's going on?" he said. He looked up. "Celeste?... Celeste?... Where'd she go?"

"Oh, don't worry about her," the nurse said. "She'll come around. If she doesn't, then she doesn't deserve a hero like you for a boyfriend. Oh, I forgot. Look over there. That Old Man left you a gift." She picked up a small, wrapped package from the seat of a chair and read the tag. "It's for you and Celeste, actually, but since she left... Well, here, I'll open it for you." She tore the paper and opened the box. "Well I'll be, look at this." She pulled a little sprig of mistletoe out of the box and held it up by its string. "Celeste doesn't know what she's missing, does she?" She went over to the metal tree holding the bags of intravenous solutions and looped it over a branch. "For when Celeste comes back," the nurse said. "Or, the next lucky young gal that walks through that door."

And a young woman did come through that door right after that. But she didn't walk. A nurse pushed her in a wheelchair. She wore a hospital gown and was holding a newborn baby in her lap. She stood, and when she laid eyes on him, she cried, "Oh, Jack Smith! Jack Smith!" She placed her baby on his chest and he instinctively pulled his arms up to cradle it.

Maria kissed him on the cheek, then held his bandaged arms in her hands and kissed the stumps. She pressed his arms against her breast, looked deeply into his eyes and started talking in Spanish. When she finished, she looked at the nurse who had come with her. The nurse said, "She wants you to know she's forever grateful for what you've done... and you're her Santo Remero—if I'm translating correctly that means something like 'holy oarsman.' And you'll always have a home in Bolonia... I guess that's in Spain, where she's from. I'm from Spanish Harlem, so what would I know? Oh, and she says she named her baby after you: Jack Smith."

Nurse Landers took the clipboard from the foot of the bed. "Jack Smith?" she said, looking at him quizzically. "That's your name?"

"It was, for a while," he said.

"Well," she said, "If my name was Chickamauga I might be looking for an alias too, especially when there are strange young women with babies hanging around. Or should I just call you 'Dad'?"

"What? Wait! I... I'm not the father."

The nurse winked at him. "Sure. Whatever you say, Pops." She made a gesture of zipping her lips and throwing away the key.

Maria wobbled and seemed dizzy. "Come on," her nurse said. "Let's get you and your baby back to your room so you can rest." She guided Maria back into the wheelchair and laid the baby in her arms. As she started to push the wheelchair out the door, she turned and said, "Oh, and Merry Christmas! Hope everybody got what they wished for."

He lay back with his forearms up, staring at the bandages. "Santiago," he whispered as his sight went blurry with tears.

12. The Relic

FOR A LONG TIME THE OLD MAN STOOD THERE, staring at his hands still gripping the oar handles, lying on a bed of white satin in their ornate little coffin. Maria held his left arm, Father Carlos his right. Without them he would have collapsed to the floor of the sacristy from the tremors that wracked his body and buckled his knees.

The relics swam through tears that pooled in his eyes and dribbled down his cheeks, but he could see them distinctly enough to remember. And his memories, too, swam like sinners pleading for their lives in the angry floodwaters outside the ark. The hours he pulled on the oars, his pain and fear of the gathering ice that gave way to gratitude for the numbness and the ability to hold on for another stroke, and another and another uncounted. The aching strain in his arms and back relieved by the mysterious warmth emanating from Maria and the baby behind him. The cries of the baby when he stopped singing, the holy quiet when he began again. The steady beat of the oars on the water, the rhythm of rowing, like a heartbeat, like breathing. Never turning around, never looking at Maria and the baby, never searching for the Old Man's lights, never checking on Santiago, and never giving in to the temptations of the ship lights receding abaft or to the puttering sound of the Chief's lifeboat engine, or his bullhorn, or the sweeping beam of his flashlight, or his gunshots in the night.

"You never doubted your faith, or your hope, or your charity, Jack Smith, my Santo Remero," Maria was saying. And as she kissed the tears from his cheeks she told him of her son, el Doctor Jack Smith Montoya, and how he yearned to be a surgeon and a healer from his boyhood, and how he had such exquisitely sensitive hands that could perform medical miracles on the poor and destitute with scalpel and suture. And as she told the old man how her son inherited his calling and his servant's heart *from you, Jack Smith, from you,* he could not help but hear the lamentations of the drowning swimmers around the ark, and their cries of regret about never being able to play the guitar, or swing a baseball bat, or feel a woman's breasts or caress her hair—not with these god-damned stumps, and not with those god-damned metal hooks he wore for so long.

And as Maria told him one story after another of how the good doctor cured the child with the hidden tumor, the pianist with the mangled hand, the breech baby with the umbilical cord wrapped around her neck, he remembered the hungry old woman in the hobo camp who strangled on a piece of meat because he could not lock his hands for a proper Heimlich maneuver. And he remembered his frustration as he tried and failed to drown his sorrow because he could not open the bottle of cheap, fortified wine that the old woman would have opened for him, but she was lying there, dead, her eyes bulging and her bloated tongue sticking out of her mouth.

And as Maria told him of the poet who was cured of his heroin addiction, and the painter of his palsy, and the buck-toothed girl of her rape-induced sleep phobia, and all by the laying on of the hands of El Santo Remero, the holy oarsman, the relic, he could not help but remember how even the most inept pickpockets saw in him an easy mark for the cash from the disability payments he carried in his pockets, and how embarrassing and difficult it was for him just to eat a god-damned sandwich or a bowl of soup-kitchen broth on his own.

And when the young man, Emilio Santiago, said that he only really truly learned to play the guitar after he was cured of his performance anxiety by a touch of the hands of El Santo Remero, the old man felt the black bile surge up from his spleen, burning his esophagus as it raised a prayer of damnation, "Santiago! You son of a bitch! You promised me a guitar lesson then you took my hands, you lying thief, you devil-bastard! You took my god-damned hands! You ruined my life! And for what? For what, Santiago! For this... for this stubborn girl... All she had to do was eat her... All she had..." But like all the other damned sinners knocking on the gopherwood, his curse drowned, leaving only the sound of the wind in his hollows, whispering, "Forgive them all."

Which somehow came out translated as: "I need a drink."

He felt a huge hand gently pat him on the shoulder and a voice behind him said, "Why not? It's Christmas." When he turned to look at the hand, the long white whiskers hanging down from above tickled his nose. With his other hand, the Old Man reached over Chick's shoulder into a hidden, inner pocket of the ancient pea coat and pulled out a small Bible. "How 'bout that," he said. There was a hole in the front cover, and something metallic filling the hole. Reaching around Chick from behind to hold the book in both hands, the Old Man leafed through the pages, revealing the bullet lodged in it.

He flicked his finger and the bullet fell into the relic box. The Old Man tapped the place on the page the bullet did not pierce, but made a deep impression. He read: *Let my prayer be set forth before thee as incense; and the lifting up of my hands as the evening sacrifice.* "Whaddya think, Chick?" he said. "Mumbo jumbo or what?"

"Pretty sure I felt something else in there," the Old Man said. He laid the book in the box and reached back into the inner pocket of the pea coat. "Yup..." He pulled out a tiny bottle with a handwritten label that, once faded, now clearly bore the words: toadstool-in-wormwood. "Jackpot," he said.

The Old Man flicked the stopper out of the bottle with his thumb. He said, "Bottoms up, down the hatch," then tilted the bottle up and drained the elixir into the old man's mouth.

Chick Charles smacked his lips and turned to look up at the Old Man. Wiping his mouth with the sleeve of his pea coat he said, "Don't you want some?"

The Old Man pulled a silver flask from his own coat pocket and replied, "Nah, I'm a peppermint schnapps man, myself," and took deep swig.

Then he put his arm around the smaller man's shoulders and said, "Come on, Chick, we got things to do." The Old Man led him out of the sacristy and down the aisle between the pews. The parishioners crossed themselves and clasped their hands together in prayer. As they stepped out the front door into the sunlight a roaring cheer and applause thundered from the huge throng of pilgrims. "Feast your eyes, Chick. Ain't it grand?" the Old Man said. "Andalusian war horses, my old friend, the finest in the world." Down on the cobblestone street below them a team of six horses stood hitched to a wagon loaded with colorfully wrapped gifts. Steam blew from the horses' nostrils into the winter air as they tossed their manes and stamped their hooves.

The two men descended the steps amid shouts and cheers and waving hats. The Old Man climbed onto the wagon bench and pulled the other up to sit next to him. With a hearty laugh he snapped the reins and the team of horses began to pull. As they moved through the streets the Old Man reached back into the wagon bed and tossed out gifts and sweets to the children, and pink envelopes with Christmas cards and money inside to the beggars and the streetwalkers and the day laborers, and to all the hollowed-out relics and invisible martyrs whose sainthood only he could see.

They came to an intersection and he pulled back on the reins and called, "Whoa, hosses!" With a grin and a nod of his head the Old Man gestured to the side of the street.

Chick turned to look in that direction. A young woman, beautiful as ever, her chestnut hair pulled back in a ponytail, stood on the sidewalk, looking up at them, smiling. "Celeste?" he said.

"Hi, Chick," she said, and she laughed, and her laughter was like wind chimes tinkling in his ears and butterflies tickling his chest, and he laughed too.

The Old Man nudged him with his elbow. "Why don't you help her aboard?" So Chickamauga Antietam Jack Smith Charles reached down, and took her hand in his, and he pulled her up onto the seat next to him.

The Old Man clicked his tongue and said, "Hah!" and the horses clip-clopped across the intersection. Chick looked down to where he was holding both of Celeste's hands in both of his. Then he looked into her eyes. She looked upward, and his eyes followed. Above them was a sprig of mistletoe, dangling from a string tied to the tip of the Old Man's slender horsewhip. They kissed and he felt infinitely light, and the clunking of the horseshoes and wagon wheels on the cobblestones gave way to a smooth, swaying motion as the Old Man drove the wagon up into the sea-blue Andalusian sky.

THE END

About Little White Cabin

Little White Cabin, LLC publishes "stories, songs, & marvels" that inform, entertain, and inspire. Find us on the internet at littlewhitecabin.com, where you can meet our artists and discover their original books, essays, short fiction, a podcast, music, and a blog.

The Relic can also be purchased in eBook and audiobook formats.

The Book of Cain, a "psycho-spiritual thriller" by Jeff Lowe, is available in paperback, eBook, and audiobook formats.

Our podcast, *A New York Yankee in the Heart of Dixie*, hosted by Oscar Bronx, can be streamed or downloaded from our website, and from Soundcloud and iTunes.

littlewhitecabin.com

www.ingramcontent.com/pod-product-compliance
Lightning Source LLC
Chambersburg PA
CBHW030458130626
46549CB00007B/2774